Author: Casey W. Christofferson
Project Manager: Zach Glazar
Editor: Jeff Harkness
Fifth Edition Conversion: Edwin Nagy
Art Direction: Casey Christofferson
Layout and Graphic Design: Charles A. Wright
Cover Design: Charles A. Wright
Cover Art: Adrian Landeros
Interior Art: Adrian Landeros
Cartography: Robert Altbauer
Fantasy Grounds Conversion: Michael G. Potter

ISBN: 978-1-62283-872-1

Frog God Games is:

Bill Webb, Matthew J. Finch, Zach Glazar, Charles A. Wright, Edwin Nagy, Mike Badolato, John Barnhouse

Table of Contents

THE TOWER OF JHEDOPHAR

INTRODUCTION

The Tower of Jhedophar is an adventure designed for four to six tier 3 characters, although it is easily scaled for higher or lower levels with slight modifications. For suggestions on how to scale the adventure, see the **Scaling the Adventure** sidebar. The adventure has several difficult traps that only a skilled rogue may bypass or remove. It is therefore suggested that at least one character be a rogue, and that the party also include one cleric or druid, and one arcane spellcaster. The remainder of the party should consist of frontline fighters or multi-classed characters.

FINDING YOUR WAY AROUND

The module starts with the background behind the story, and then gives a short synopsis of the expected adventure that your party will have. Before the description of the adventure locations, a few options for hooking your players are given. Throughout the adventure description, you will magic items and spells in italics. Those with a superscript A can be found in Appendix A, while the remainder should be found in a fifth edition SRD of your choice. Creatures are in bold where encountered. Those with a superscript can be found in Appendix B while the rest should be available in the SRD.

BACKGROUND

The Tower of Jhedophar was once a great school of magic where the arch-mage Jhedophar trained many of the age's greatest wizards and sorcerers in the arcane arts. Times changed — as did Jhedophar — and as the half-elf finally felt the weariness of age creep into his bones, he began frantically to strive as many wizards do for means to unnaturally lengthen his life. Such is the fate of wizards to possess the power to bind planes and the mysteries of existence with words, alchemy, and the secret numbers that are the root of the universe. Vexing it must be to have so many wonders to discover yet only a limited lifespan with which to uncover even greater knowledge.

Jhedophar was once a great hero who, with the aid of Lord Tork and other great heroes, wrested the *mandrake staff*[A] from the witches of Stench-Hollow Downs. Many adventures did he have, the strange *mandrake staff* figuring greatly in the building of his legend, and some say that the fame of his exploits indeed contributed to the success of his school of magic. At some point, however, something changed in Jhedophar, turning his heart to evil. Some say it was the power of the *mandrake staff*, while others claim it was contact with a dark force he discovered while walking the planes of creation.

For whatever reason, 800 years ago, or so the legend says, Jhedophar wrought a great ritual within the summoning chamber of his tower and made contact with a being of pure evil whose will and mind were greater than his own. There, Jhedophar was granted immortality in un-death by the might of this unspeakable power. Jhedophar signed and sealed the pact with the blood of his very own apprentices.

Always fearful of thieves, Jhedophar constructed a great covered labyrinth around the base of his tower, girding it from outside intrusions. This labyrinth that guards the entrance to the tower is nearly as legendary as the tower itself, having been the bane of many a treasure seeker or would-be plunderer of the secrets that Jhedophar hath wrought within his eldritch fortress.

Beyond the construction of the labyrinth and the sealing of the great portal, little is known of what goes on within the gleaming tower. It is believed that Jhedophar is a great traveler of the planes and a frequent visitor to the City of Brass. Speculation being what it is, one fact remains: Jhedophar was the bearer of the *mandrake staff*, a unique staff said to possess unlimited power in the hands of its wielder.

SYNOPSIS

Having heard of the great wonders hidden within the Tower of Jhedophar, the characters seek out the structure to plunder its vast resources of magical knowledge and to destroy the powerful evil which the very existence of Jhedophar represents. The characters travel a great distance through tangled wilderness or over rough and stormy seas (at your discretion) to finally reach the fabled Tower of Jhedophar. Once there, they enter the Labyrinth of Jhedophar that girds the tower's exterior. The characters face down new adversaries and traps before they enter the tower's forbidden portals and peruse its secrets.

After encountering undead creatures known as **spellgorged zombies**[B], the characters finally face Jhedophar, where the lich attempts to dissuade them from destroying him by asking the characters to rid him of a red dragon that has taken up residence in his labyrinth. The party may have already made the same deal with the dragon, who is attempting to gain the fabled *mandrake staff* for himself!

Upon completing the adventure, the characters gain a new powerful magic item and knowledge of new magical spells. It is possible the characters may gain the sword known as *Karelis*[A], a weapon that may be used as a seed for further adventure.

SCALING THE ADVENTURE

The following adjustments could be made to raise or lower the difficulty of the adventure.

FOR LOWER-LEVEL CHARACTERS

- Reduce the number of Random Encounters, or delete them from the adventure entirely
- Change bloody bones[B] to normal skeletons.
- Change demiurge[B] to a wraith.
- Change Exeterus[B] to a young red dragon or a red dragon wyrmling.
- Change Lord Tork's[B] *+2 shield* into a nonmagical shield and his AC to 22.
- Make Jhedophar's Constitution score 16, his hit points 135, and remove his *spell scrolls*.

FOR HIGHER-LEVEL CHARACTERS

- Change bloody bones[B] to mummies.
- Increase the demiurge's[B] Constitution score to 18 and its hit points to 102.
- Change Exeterus to an ancient red dragon.
- Make Lord Tork's Constitution score 16 and his hit points 161.
- Increase the hit points of the spellgorged zombies[B].
- Make Jhedophar's Constitution score 20 and his hit points 171.

Adventure Hooks

The characters may find their way to the Tower of Jhedophar by various routes. Since it has no set location, you may insert the Tower of Jhedophar into your campaign wherever you desire. It could be located in an evil city, in a ruin, on an island, in a lost jungle, or high up on a mountaintop. Any wilderness adventures of appropriate difficulty to lead the characters to the tower are your domain. Listed below are adventure hooks designed to get the characters immediately involved in the adventure.

• While traveling from one place to another, the characters discover they are passing close to the Tower of Jhedophar. Appropriate Intelligence (Arcana) checks offer clues about the fall of Jhedophar and the possible secrets hidden within his tower.

• Villagers beseech the characters to seek out and destroy a dragon that is laired within the cursed Tower of Jhedophar. They tell of a band of heroes who went forth over a month ago to slay the dragon but never returned.

• A treasure map describes a fabulous magical item called the *mandrake staff*[A] and its supposed location in a place called the Tower of Jhedophar.

• A cleric character is sent by his religious order to bring back the *mandrake staff*[A] from the clutches of Jhedophar so that its power may be investigated. This plot device works equally well for wizards, who are sent instead by their guild. Alternatively, a wizard's guild could send the characters to seek revenge on Jhedophar for murdering his apprentices.

• A paladin's order, ranger's troupe, or barbarian's clan sends the characters out in search of the lost sword *Karelis*[A] that is said to have belonged to the famed knight known as Lord Tork. The sword is destined to help thwart a great evil soon coming to the world.

The Labyrinth of Jhedophar

The labyrinth of Jhedophar was constructed to keep would-be thieves from bothering his delicate arcane studies. It serves as the lair to his undead minions and protectors such as Nazoj the demiurge[B] and E'elaim the crypt thing[B]. The adult red dragon Exeterus also makes his home here. He is an uninvited squatter residing in the western side of the labyrinth. The characters must navigate this dangerous labyrinth to find the actual entrance to the Tower of Jhedophar, possibly enlisting the aid of the spirits and monsters within the labyrinth to accomplish their goal. Of course, we all know that's not going to happen, and the characters will instead crawl from this adventure covered in blood and gore.

> A broad disk-shaped structure girds the base of the Tower of Jhedophar. A pair of solid bronze doors twenty feet wide in the southern face of the tower appears to be the only entrance. Like the tower itself, the sides of the disk are as smooth as glass, affording no handholds. The entire surface of the central tower and the disk around its base give off a strange luminescence that seems to change with the play of light from the sun and moon.

The tower obviously cannot be climbed without magical means. Characters choosing to climb using *spider climb* or who *levitate* or *fly* to the top of the disk note that the roof is broken along the southwestern edge of the disk. The disk is 270 feet in diameter and 20 feet tall, with the tower rising from the center of the disk itself.

The entry portals are solid two-inch-thick bronze and locked with an *arcane lock* spell and a mechanical lock. Each has an AC of 18 and 80 hit points, and can be opened with a successful DC 27 Strength check or DC 23 Dexterity check with thieves' tools if the *arcane lock* is in effect.

The Labyrinth of Jhedophar

Entrances and Exits: Area L-1 in the south of the tower complex; roof opening in **Area L-11**.

Wandering Monsters: The animated remains of many unlucky adventurers scour much of the labyrinth in search of food. Roll 1d12 once every 30 minutes the characters spend within the labyrinth.

1d12	Encounter
1	1d2 wraiths
2	1d4 + 1 bloody bones[B]
3	1d4 spectres
4	1d2 ghouls (minotaur)[B]
5	2d4 four-armed gargoyles[B]
6	1d4 barrow wights[B]
7–12	No encounter

Shielding. The labyrinth is shielded from teleportation and dimensional travel into it. However, it is not shielded from teleportation out of the labyrinth. Jhedophar may enter and exit the labyrinth as he pleases, which is to say, he does not, traveling directly to his chambers in his tower and avoiding the goings on within the labyrinth altogether.

Continuous Effects. The entire labyrinth is affected as if by a *desecrate*[A] spell that strengthens the power of the undead creatures dwelling within it. Any creature slain within the labyrinth rises as a bloody bones[B] in 1d6 rounds. If a spellcaster begins to cast *raise dead* or *resurrection* on a slain creature before the 1d6 rounds pass and the spell is successfully completed, the creature does not become undead.

Standard Features. Unless otherwise noted, all doors within the labyrinth of Jhedophar are locked and made of two-inch-thick bronze. Each has an AC of 18 and 60 hit points and can be opened with a successful DC 20 Strength check or DC 18 Dexterity check with thieves' tools. Nazoj the demiurge (area **L-10**) and E'elaim the crypt thing (area **L-17**) hold *wardstones of Jhedophar*[A] that open all the doors inside the labyrinth and the tower.

L-1. Entrance Chamber

> The entrance chamber is barren except for glowing words inlaid with silver upon the back wall of the chamber. Exits are to the east and west.

When read, the writing on the wall instantly transforms into a tongue the reader easily comprehends. It says: "Be gone fools who tread within the labyrinth of Jhedophar; from here my tower door is too far. Sad it was the day you chose to invade my home and thus here forever will reside thy bones."

As soon as the characters enter the labyrinth, Jhedophar casts a *wall of stone* (on which he maintains concentration until it becomes permanent) over the doorway to block their escape. He has been scrying their progress with his *crystal ball*.

L-2. BLOODY BONES

Five **bloody bones**[B] sit on the floor throwing dice and gambling over a pile of gold coins. They attack when the characters enter the chamber.

Remember to include the effects of the labyrinth's continuous *desecrate*[A] spell on all undead.

Treasure: The bloody bones have 300 gp that they have been passing back and forth to one another as they mindlessly gambled away the ages.

L-3. SPIKED PIT TRAP

Stepping on the floor plate in this corner triggers a locking spiked pit trap. The pit is 10 feet wide by 10 feet long by 20 feet deep. A successful DC 15 Wisdom (Perception) allows characters to notice a lack of traffic on the lid of the pit. A successful DC 15 Intelligence (Investigation) check is needed to confirm it as a trap. The use of thieves' tools and successful DC 15 Dexterity check will disable the mechanism. Finally, a successful DC 20 Strength check is necessary to pry open the sealed pit. Any creature falling into the trap take falling damage plus 11 (2d10) piercing damage from spikes. The trap resets automatically in one minute.

L-4. Trapper

A large, ornately carved chest sitting in the center of this broad, irregularly shaped room is a **trapper**[B]. The creature waits until the majority of the party crosses into the center of the room to attack.

L-5. Ten Pin Alley

A trapped floor plate triggers a two-part *hold monster* and rolling sphere trap Jhedophar set long ago while he was in one of his crueler moods. A character succeeding on a DC 22 Wisdom (Perception) check notices something off about the stone around the pressure plate. Searching the floor for traps and succeeding on a DC 20 Intelligence (Investigation) check identifies the pressure plate for this subtle device. When triggered by 20 or more pounds of pressure, *hold monster* (spell save DC 20) is cast on up to five creatures within a 10-foot radius of the trigger plate. Then, within seconds, a giant stone ball hidden behind an illusory wall to the north rolls down the hallway, crushing all within its path. Each creature in the path must succeed on a DC 15 Dexterity saving throw or take 55 (10d10) bludgeoning damage and be knocked prone. A character using thieves' tools and succeeding on a DC 20 Dexterity check can disable the trap mechanism. Once sprung, the entire trap magically resets after 10 minutes. The illusory wall can be seen for what it is with a successful DC 20 Intelligence (Investigation) check.

Note: Held characters get no saving throw against damage caused by the giant stone ball.

L-6. Crypt of Lord Tork

One round after characters enter the chamber, the sepulcher's lid slides free, and the **skeleton warrior**[B] that was once Lord Tork rises from his tomb. In life, Lord Tork was a great hero, a cavalier without measure among the horsemen of his age. He was also Jhedophar's ally and swore to protect the wizard for all the days of his life. He even granted Jhedophar the land upon which the tower is built. However, Lord Tork never expected the depths to which the wizard's greed and lust for knowledge would take him. When word came that Jhedophar sealed the school and slew his apprentices, Lord Tork rode forth upon his valiant steed Jasper to challenge the wizard.

The vigilant Jhedophar was prepared for the aging hero, however, and slew Lord Tork, binding his soul to a circlet of gold. Jhedophar now controls the poor hero's bones from his scrying chamber, forcing the long-ago hero to serve as a guardian to the wizard's lair.

Remember to include the effects of the labyrinth's continuous *desecrate*[A] spell on all undead.

Tactics: Lord Tork apologizes for his actions but attacks the characters relentlessly and ruthlessly. He tries to avoid allowing the characters gang up on him. He uses his Disarm ability to neutralize the biggest threats. Lord Tork uses his *boots of striding and springing* to attempt to maneuver himself into a position where he need only face one or two characters at a time so that he may focus his deadly blows. As Lord Tork faces his eventual destruction, he regains a moment of control and the memory of his former life. He bequeaths *Karelis*[A] to his most honorable opponent with the following words: "Take her and defend her as she defends thee; may you complete the task which I failed."

Note: If the characters somehow find a way to free Lord Tork from his servitude by gaining the golden circlet from Jhedophar, grant each of them a 1,000 XP story award bonus. Should the characters cast *true resurrection* upon the dust that was once Lord Tork, his ashes rise as a **knight** in his mid-fifties with 78 hit points and an AC based on his magical armor and equipment. While wielding the fabled blade *Karelis*[A], Lord Tork is dashing and brave. Seeing the characters as great and noble allies, he offers to join them in defeating Jhedophar and Exeterus — if they then travel with him to the Plane of Agony to seek the Citadel of the Flayer Knights where *Karelis'* body has been imprisoned for thousands of years.

Treasure: The glinting metal in the chamber is *+1 chain barding* and *horseshoes of a zephyr* that once belonged to Jasper.

What bit of memory still resides within the skull of Lord Tork remembers the sword *Karelis*[A] well and prays that the soul within the blade may someday return to the elf maiden to whom it belongs. Although he attempted to do so in life, it was a quest he would unfortunately never fulfill.

L-7. Entry Hall to the Inner Labyrinth

An **iron golem** guarding the chamber leading to the inner labyrinth animates and attacks the characters instantly.

The portals to the inner labyrinth are 1-foot-thick stone and held with an *arcane lock* spell and locked with a mechanical lock (AC 18; HP 90; a successful DC 30 Strength check or DC 25 Dexterity check with thieves' tools will open it while the *arcane lock* is in place; if the *arcane lock* is neutralized, only a successful DC 20 Strength check or DC 15 Dexterity check with thieves' tools is required).

L-8. Rue Mohrgs Morgue

This chamber is guarded by 3 **mohrgs**[B] that attack the characters as soon as they enter the chamber. Remember to include the effects of the labyrinth's continuous *desecrate*[A] spell on all undead.

The mohrgs are made up of the bodies of greedy adventurers who sought to wrest the *mandrake staff*[A] from Jhedophar but were destroyed and turned into mohrgs after hours of torture. Their treasures have long since fallen into other hands.

L-9. One Wrong Turn

Stepping upon this floor plate triggers a scything blade trap. Putting more than 20 pounds of pressure on the plate causes three razor sharp blades to emerge from the wall and swipe horizontally across the width of the hallway between 3 and 5 feet off the ground. Any creature within 5 feet of the pressure plate when it is triggered must succeed on a DC 15 Dexterity saving throw or take 13 (3d8) slashing damage. A successful DC 16 Intelligence (Investigation) check of the floor reveals the existence of the pressure plate, and a successful DC 15 Dexterity check with thieves' tools disarms it.

L-10. Nazoj's Chamber (or You're Not on the List!)

The demonic trappings of a fallen priest adorn this small chamber, and the ghost-like image of a being twisted with evil rises from the shadows.

This is Nazoj the **demiurge**[B].

He turns toward any priest or paladin and laughs cruelly. He asks, "So, are you on the list?" The creature looks over a parchment that crumbles to dust in its ghost-like hands. "No. It doesn't appear as if you are on the list after all. Truly too bad for you, but if you aren't on the list, Jhedophar says I have to kill you. I have fallen far in service to Jhedophar. So too shall you fall in the name of our dread queen Beluiri." With that, Nazoj shakes his head and says, "Besides, if you're not on the list, you're just not on the list." He then attacks.

Remember to include the effects of the labyrinth's continuous *desecrate*[A] spell on all undead.

Tactics. The demiurge uses his Transfixing Gaze on heavily armed and armored opponents so that he may use his Soul Touch ability to fly through them and slay them with ease. He next turns his attention to clerics and wizards to finish them off before they can harm him.

A doorway in the eastern wall leads to **Area L-18** of the inner labyrinth.

Treasure. The skeletal remains of three of the demiurge's previous victims bear the following items: a *ring of resistance* (fire), a *cursed chain shirt* that appears as a *+1 chain shirt* but actually grants −1 to the wearer's armor class, a suit of *+1 scale mail*, and the *wardstone of Jhedophar*[A].

Note: The *wardstone of Jhedophar* allows free passage through the *arcane locked* doors of the Tower of Jhedophar without triggering any of the curses or traps upon them — with the exception of the doors to Jhedophar's personal chambers. Jhedophar left the *wardstone* with the demiurge as he knows Nazoj would give the stone only to someone who knows him well and is on legitimate business.

L-11. Lair of Exeterus

The stench of snakes and sulfur fill this huge chamber. As the light from your torches stretches into the chamber, the glow reflects off a pair of great eyes burning like red-hot coals as they turn in your direction. Arcane chanting can be heard from the bowels of the chamber. A voice calls out to you: "Who dares enter the lair of Exeterus and disturb his musings? Speak quickly, mammals, or I shall gleefully feast upon your paltry offerings."

At this point, **Exeterus**[B] the adult red dragon partially reveals himself to the characters. The characters must talk or act quickly, or all is lost. Exeterus, like most of his loathsome kind, is a smart and deadly opponent. Should the characters impress Exeterus with the proper amount of pandering to his might and power, the red dragon makes his play, suggesting that the characters retrieve the *mandrake staff*[A] for him. In return, he shall spare their meager lives.

If asked why he has not simply taken the staff, he scoffs and explains that the mighty lich Jhedophar has been too frightened to come down from his high tower and face the dragon's wrath. This is partially true. Jhedophar does indeed fear Exeterus, for he knows that while he could possibly destroy the dragon, the dragon has better than even odds of destroying him as well. Jhedophar figures that Exeterus makes a good guardian for his labyrinth, and so he simply ignores the upstart dragon. Should the characters agree to destroy Jhedophar and bring Exeterus the *mandrake staff*[A], the dragon tells them exactly where a pass key for all the doors in the tower and labyrinth is located (a *wardstone of Jhedophar* in **Area L-10** with Nazoj the Demiurge).

Of course, Exeterus has no intention of keeping his part of the bargain. Should the characters destroy Jhedophar, he greedily accepts the staff from them and then attempts to destroy them. Furthermore, should the characters attempt to sneak off without giving him the staff, he stops at nothing to hunt them down until they are destroyed or he is.

Tactics. The vision the characters see when they enter is not actually Exeterus but a *silent image* that the *invisible* Exeterus stands behind. If the party makes too much noise in **Areas L-12** or **L-13** Exeterus is waiting for them with these spells in place when they arrive.

If the characters arrive looking for a fight, Exeterus breathes upon them. He follows by casting *slow* on lightly armored foes and *charm person* on heavily armored ones. Once he starts taking damage, he continues breathing fire on rounds that he can and focuses on individual targets, seeking to slay one after another until all the characters are dead. Should any attempt to escape, Exeterus casts *scrying* to discern their location and mercilessly hunts them down. If necessary, he casts *charm person* on the party's rogue to get him sneak attacking his buddies instead.

Treasure: Exeterus' treasure hoard contains the following items: a *+2 shield*, a *ring of greater protection*[A], a *cursed ring of wizardry*[A]. There is also a *staff of healing*, a *spell wand*[A] of *ice storm*, a *+2 greatsword*, a *spell wand*[A] of *magic weapon*, a *ring of three wishes* with one *wish* remaining, and a pair of *eyes of petrification*[A]. Exeterus also has 16,000 gp worth of various coins, and 3,450 gp worth of gems, jewelry, and fine art.

L-12. Lartugi's Chamber

Lartugi[B] was once a famous halfling rogue who specialized in raiding and plundering the towers of several wizards throughout the world. That was until he took the left turn upon entering the labyrinth of Jhedophar and came face to face with Exeterus. Now, Lartugi is Exeterus' thrall, valet, and spokesperson when the dragon wishes to be left undisturbed. Exeterus keeps Lartugi constantly under the effects of *charm person* and *suggestion* spells. He gave Lartugi some valuables from his treasure hoard to keep the halfling satisfied.

Lartugi is fairly intelligent but totally in the thrall of his dragon master, whom he defends to the death.

If the party made lots of noise fighting the gargoyles in **Area L-14**, Lartugi hides and sneaks up to just outside **Area L-13** to observe them. Lartugi then slips behind them with his enormous hide ability and waits for them to meet his master Exeterus. Should the characters fight Exeterus, Lartugi remains in the shadows (and out of the way of Exeterus' breath weapon). If the characters take the deal, he tails them through the maze and tower, possibly aiding them as silently and quietly as he can while they fight Jhedophar.

Treasure. Lartugi, a thief through and through, hid his treasure (excluding what he carries on his person) within his chamber under a loose flagstone that requires a success on a DC 20 Intelligence (Investigation) check to detect. In the hollow under the stone is a bag of gemstones worth 900 gp and a sack with 100 pp in it.

L-13. Watch Your Step

A hidden pit trap lies here. It is 10 feet wide by 10 feet long by 60 feet deep. A successful DC 15 Wisdom (Perception) will allow characters to notice something abnormal about the pit's cover. A successful DC 15 Intelligence (Investigation) check confirms it as a pit trap, while using thieves' tools and succeeding on a DC 15 Dexterity check disables the hinge and prevents the cover from falling open. The trap is triggered by the first person to cross over the covering but doesn't activate until another being crosses. Thus, any scouts can pass over it with ease, but those following are in danger. The trap must be manually reset.

A patch of **phycomid**[B] grows upon the bones of a dead rogue at the bottom of the pit. Among the rogue's possessions are a set of thieves' tools and a *+2 dagger*. The rest of the rogue's armor and equipment have long since rotted away. Casting *speak with dead* upon the rogue

reveals that his name was Yadre and that he was a servant of the infamous Underguild. His masters sent him to steal the *mandrake staff*[A] in exchange for a promise of immortality.

The phycomid fires its acidic Fluid Globule at the first victim to fall into the pit as soon as the creature lands.

L-14. Gargoyles' Lair

This chamber is home to 12 **four-armed gargoyles**[B] and an advanced margoyle known as **Grytis**[B]. The 13 line the walls of the chamber, frozen, making it impossible to notice that the creatures are actually alive. Grytis and his brethren wait until the characters are in the center of the room to attack.

Tactics. The gargoyles gang up on individual characters, with three groups of four attacking one character at a time, intent on destroying them. If the party makes lots of noise in **Area L-1**, the gargoyles cover themselves in *adherer oil*[A] that Exeterus gave them. The gargoyles worship Exeterus and make as much noise as they can while fighting. They may even disengage from combat to warn the dragon. For years, a disgusted Jhedophar has attempted to eradicate the gargoyles from the labyrinth's foyer, only to have them return whenever he is off visiting the planes of existence.

L-15. Entrance to the Inner Labyrinth

A pair of **barrow wights**[B] guard the true entrance to the inner labyrinth. The barrow wights immediately attack.

A hallway to the southeast leads deeper into the labyrinth.

L-16. Death from Above

A pressure plate in the floor triggers a falling block trap. If triggered, the only true path to the labyrinth is permanently sealed off, requiring a *passwall* or similar spell to bypass it. Additionally, all creatures in the spaces under the block (see Map 1: Labyrinth of Jhedophar) must succeed on a DC 15 Dexterity saving throw or take 21 (6d6) bludgeoning damage. The trigger plate can be found with a successful DC 15 Intelligence (Investigation) check, and the trap can be disarmed with the use of thieves' tools and a successful DC 17 Dexterity check.

L-17. E'elaim's Chamber

Once a sorceress and ally of Jhedophar, the **crypt thing**[B] that remains is filled with spite and cruelty although she is not necessarily evil. E'elaim is bound to the power of Jhedophar for all eternity. She sits upon a throne fit for a queen, carved from brilliantly polished vermillion wood inlaid with gold and precious jewels. She uses her powers of teleportation to cast intruders from the entrance of Jhedophar's tower as she clacks her dusty jaws in a mockery of laughter.

Remember to include the effects of the labyrinth's continuous *desecrate*[A] spell on all undead.

Tactics. E'elaim attempts to teleport creatures within 50 feet of her in random directions throughout the labyrinth. She then flees into the tower to avoid the characters' subsequent assault, laughing hysterically all the while.

Treasure. The throne that the crypt thing sits upon is made of precious hardwoods and gold. It weighs just over 70 pounds and is worth approximately 700 gp to a collector in a large city. E'elaim also holds a *wardstone of Jhedophar*[A] that she created that opens all the doors in the labyrinth and the tower (except for the lich's quarters on the eighth floor).

Teleport Locations

When E'elaim teleports a character, roll 1d20 on the table below to see where the target ends up. This result could prove quite deadly to characters, so handle the encounter with care.

1d20	Location
1	Area L-1. Entrance Chamber
2	Area L-2. Bloody Bones
3	Area L-3. Spiked Pit Trap
4	Area L-4. Trapper
5	Area L-5. Ten Pin Alley
6	Area L-6. Crypt of Lord Tork
7	Area L-7. Entry Hall to the Inner Labyrinth
8	Area L-8. Rue Mohrgs Morgue
9	Area L-9. One Wrong Turn
10	Area L-10. Nazoj's Chamber
11	Area L-11. Lair of Exeterus
12	Area L-12. Lartugi's Chamber
13	Area L-13. Watch Your Step
14	Area L-14. Gargoyles' Lair
15	Area L-15. Entrance to the Inner Labyrinth
16	Area L-16. Death from Above
17	Outside the labyrinth
18	Area L-18. False Entrance to the Tower
19	Area L-19. Crypts of the Barrow Wights
20	Area L-20. Shadow and Shadow Rats' Nests

Note: It is possible that characters may be teleported outside the labyrinth. Furthermore, E'elaim may simply find the characters too pesky to deal with and teleport them 1d10 x 20 feet straight up into the air. Normal falling damage minus 30 feet applies as the roof of the labyrinth is roughly 30 feet tall. This option should be reserved only for individuals who harm E'elaim. It is hoped that they are wearing *rings of feather falling* if this happens. If not, perhaps one of their allies brought a sponge and a *rod of resurrection* in her standard adventuring gear.

If characters are teleported outside the labyrinth and survive any falling damage, they are faced with the very real possibility that their allies may still be alive inside. A *wall of stone* now covers the labyrinth's door and must be dealt with before the character has any hope of rescuing those inside.

L-18. False Entrance to the Tower

The doorway to this chamber is ornately wrought bronze and gives the impression that it is an antechamber leading to the foot of the Tower of Jhedophar. Halls lead off to the north and south, obviously skirting the tower itself. Many wards are scribed upon the portal, and a character making a successful DC 20 Intelligence (Arcana) or Intelligence (Investigation) check can discover that the door is warded with a permanent *magic circle*.

Inscribed above the door is a warning that reads: "Turn ye back from the Tower of Jhedophar, or face his wrath. Let one thousand curses blister your carcasses and burn your soul to ash and soot, and a thousand years may you suffer in torment for defiling his home! Be gone thieves this is thy last warning!"

This chamber beyond the doorway is the lair of Clytos the **gharros demon**[B]. Beluiri gifted Clytos to Jhedophar as punishment when the gharros demon fell into her disfavor. Rather than destroy Clytos, she sent him to Jhedophar to do with as he wished. Of course, Clytos was recalcitrant and lazy. Having little use for Clytos other than as a guardian in his labyrinth, Jhedophar exiled the gharros demon to live within this chamber.

The wizard sealed the door with a special *magic circle* and *bestow curse* trap. Fiddling with the door breaks the *magic circle* and triggers the *bestow curse* (spell save DC 20) upon the fool tampering with the doorway. A character who fails her saving throw against this curse has disadvantage on all Dexterity checks and saving throws until the curse is negated by a *remove curse*, *dispel magic*, or similar spell. Inspecting the door and succeeding on a DC 20 Intelligence (Arcana) or Intelligence (Investigation) check detects the presence of the trap. Using thieves' tools and succeeding on a DC 20 Dexterity check disarms this magical trap.

Clytos survived all these years by summoning lesser demons and devouring them when they found themselves trapped within the *magic circle*.

Clytos bears a sentient battleaxe named *Suzette*[A] that he wields with deadly efficiency (in lieu of the gharros demon's usual halberd). He named the battleaxe in honor of the erinyes that Beluiri caught him with at a social event in the lower planes. Once the circle is broken, the demon intends to slay whomever he can in his rage at his long imprisonment. He does not leave the labyrinth, however; he knows that Jhedophar is likely to destroy him for doing so.

L-19: Crypts of the Barrow Wights

This chamber holds the crypts of 6 **barrow wights**[B] who were Lord Tork's liegemen. They came to rescue his body from Jhedophar's clutches but failed miserably and now rest here as guardians.

Each barrow wight wears plate armor (Armor Class 18) and has a *+1 greatsword* that it leaves inside its crypt. They emerge and attack as soon as characters enter.

Remember to include the effects of the labyrinth's continuous *desecrate*[A] spell on all undead.

L-20: Shadow and Shadow Rats Nest

This chamber contains a refuse heap that once housed a large colony of dire rats. A **shadow** sent by Jhedophar to clean the labyrinth of any vermin eventually stumbled upon the rats' lair. Now, the **shadow** and his pack of **shadow rats**[B] — along with his 2 spawned **shadows** — wait in the darkness for their next meal. Feasting is good every few years when another foolish party of adventurers attempts to learn the secrets of the tower.

The dire shadow rats and the shadows attack when the characters enter the chamber.

Remember to include the effects of the labyrinth's continuous *desecrate*[A] spell on all undead.

Treasure. Hidden among the detritus is a *+1 greataxe*, a *potion of healing*, and 344 gp.

The Tower of Jhedophar

The following locations are found inside the wizard's tower at the center of the labyrinth.

1-A. The Entryway

The front door of the tower is one-foot-thick stone and held with an *arcane lock* spell. The door has AC 18 and 90 hit points. A successful DC 30 Strength check or DC 25 Dexterity check with thieves' tools will open it while the *arcane lock* is in place; if the *arcane lock* is neutralized, only a successful DC 20 Strength check or DC 15 Dexterity check with thieves' tools is required. Hateful runes warn would-be thieves and trespassers away from the door.

Knock suppresses the *arcane lock* but does not protect the caster from the door's curse. Tampering with the door triggers a special *bestow curse* trap (spell save DC 20). A character who fails the saving throw against this curse has disadvantage on all Wisdom checks and saving throws until the curse is negated by a *remove curse*, *dispel magic*, or similar spell. Inspecting the door and succeeding on a DC 20 Intelligence (Arcana) or Intelligence (Investigation) check detects the presence of the trap. Using thieves' tools and succeeding on a DC 20 Dexterity check disarms this magical trap.

> The entry chamber features a portrait of Jhedophar as he appeared in life. He is dressed in his caster's robes and bears a great staff carved in a grotesque and twisted mockery of a man. Several non-magical books are on a small coffee table, and a moldy green sofa and chairs sit around it. The chamber has no windows, and a doorway leads to the north. Several inches of dust coat the sofa, chairs, and the coffee table.

1-B. The Abjuration Chamber

The first floor of the tower is a room dedicated to the school of abjuration, a guard against any who would attempt to bypass Jhedophar's normal protections.

Practitioners once studied spells here, but the thick dust on the floor indicates that such studies must surely have given way to the passage of time and neglect.

Runes are scribed on nearly every surface within this room, upon the tables and walls. Rune bindings and other symbols of protection and wards decorate scroll cases and bookshelves.

Unwarily perusing any of these volumes triggers a *ward of pain*[A] (spell save DC 20) upon the reader. The ward on a particular book can be detected with a successful DC 20 Intelligence (Investigation) check but can only be neutralized with the use of *dispel magic* or similar spell.

Two rounds after characters enter the abjuration chamber, 2 **spellgorged zombies**[B] step from the corners of the chamber and unleash a pair of *cone of cold* spells before closing for melee.

Remember to include the effects of the tower's continuous *desecrate*[A] spell on all undead.

A scroll case holds an *alarm* spell that notifies Jhedophar if it is touched. After scrying on the characters in the labyrinth with his *crystal ball*, Jhedophar assumed they were dealt with and went about his studies. Once he learns the characters breached his tower, however, Jhedophar immediately prepares to face them. He teleports to the evocation chamber (**Area 2**) and prepares to face the intruders.

One scroll case is a *scroll case of obscuring*[A]. Within it are *spell scrolls* containing the following spells:

Inside the Tower

Wandering Monsters. No wandering monsters are in the Tower of Jhedophar unless the characters let them in from the labyrinth. Instead, roll 1d10 for each level of the tower that the party enters. On a roll of 1, Jhedophar is somewhere upon that level of the tower going about his business. If the characters trigger an *alarm* spell (see **Area 1-B**) alerting Jhedophar, he will be waiting in **Area 2**.

Shielding. The Tower of Jhedophar is shielded from teleportation and dimensional travel into it. However, the shielding does not prevent teleportation out of the tower. Jhedophar may enter and exit the tower as he pleases,. The exterior walls are further shielded to be immune to the effects of *passwall*, *stone shape*, and similar spells. Casting such spells inside the tower is fine, but they do not work on the walls of the outer tower.

Continuous Effects. Due to the shrine to Beluiri, the tower is affected as if by a *desecrate*[A] spell that strengthens the power of the undead creatures dwelling within it.

Standard Features. Unless otherwise noted, all doors within the Tower of Jhedophar are locked and made of bronze (2 in. thick; AC 18; HP 60; a successful DC 20 Strength check or DC 18 Dexterity check with thieves' tools will open one). Nazoj the demiurge (area **L-10**) and E'elaim the crypt thing (area **L-17**) hold *wardstones of Jhedophar* that open all the doors in the labyrinth and the tower (with the exception of the lich's quarters on the eighth floor).

Scroll #1: *shield, arcane lock, protection from energy*
Scroll #2: *nondetection, stoneskin*
Scroll #3: *dispel magic* (5th level spell slot)

Other scrolls and tomes are filled with magical knowledge that references the school of abjuration and its uses. Carefully studying these books (requiring weeks of diligent research equal to 6 minus the character's Intelligence bonus [min 1 week]) grants the reader a permanent +2 bonus to Intelligence (Arcana) checks as they pertain to the casting of or use of abjuration spells.

A staircase leads to a warded doorway that opens onto the second floor. The staircase is guarded with a message on the door to all that would intrude upon Jhedophar's stronghold: *Read in me and be relieved! Jhedophar has no time for thieves! With these words shall you burn. For your ashes, I have an urn.*

Reading this warning immediately sets off the *glyph of warding* spell trap on the door. It can be noticed without setting it off with a successful DC 20 Intelligence (Investigation) check. The spell is aimed to blast only those standing before the doorway. The explosive fire runes version of *glyph of warding* (spell save DC 20) can be neutralized by the use of thieves' tools and a successful DC 20 Dexterity check to carefully etch out part of the symbols. The use of *dispel magic* or similar spell may also disable the glyph.

2. Evocation Chamber

The evocation chamber is a bare room with a sand pit flanked by two low 10-foot-high-by-40-foot-long walls lined with engraved silver runes. Jhedophar created illusions here for those studying evocation spells so that they could practice their skills at arcane combat. He often created encounters for novices similar to what they might encounter on an adventure, thus allowing his apprentices to blast it out in the relative safety of this room. The walls are guarded against magic so

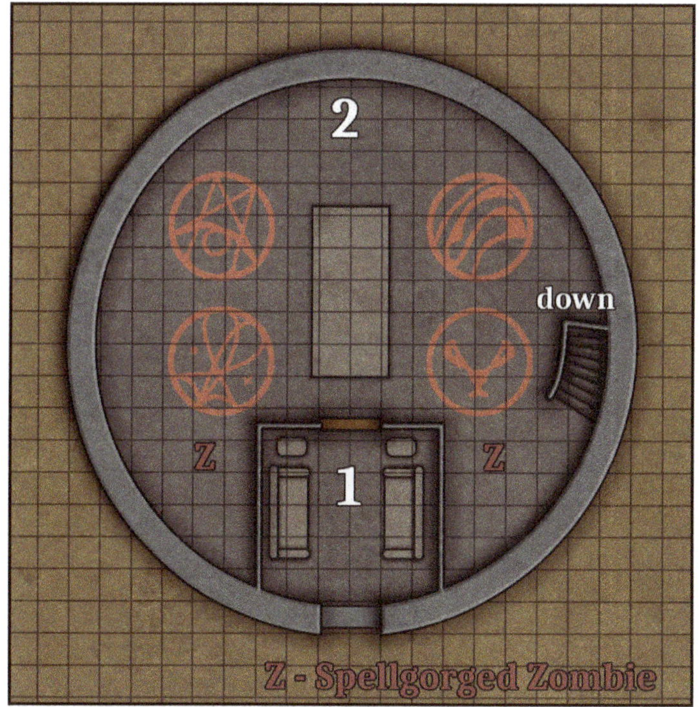

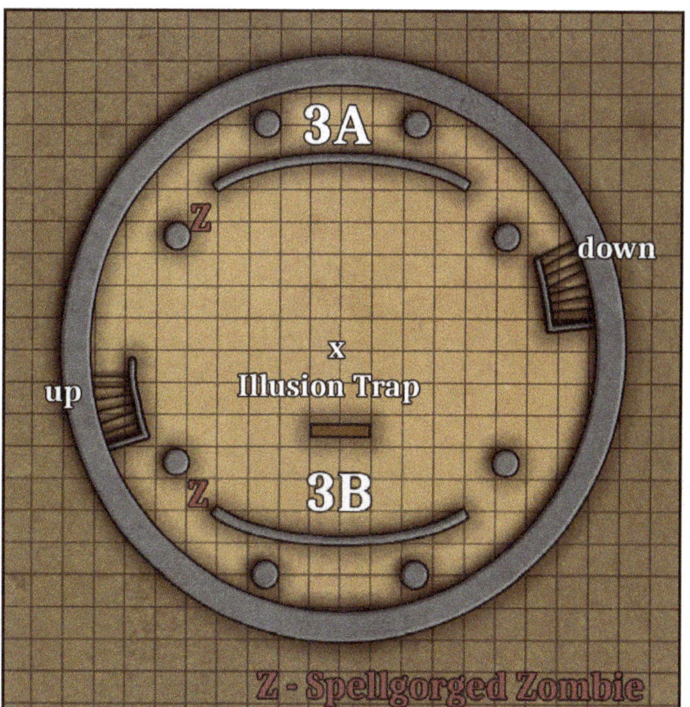

that an accidentally miscast spell does not blow debris out into the well-tended flower gardens he once kept on the roof of the labyrinth.

As the characters search the room, a pair of **spellgorged zombies**[B] attack, blasting the party with a pair of *fireballs* (5th level spell slot; spell save DC 20).

Remember to include the effects of the tower's continuous *desecrate*[A] spell on all undead.

After the fireballs explode, the zombies move forward and attack with their claws until destroyed.

The low walls flanking the sand pit are trapped with *programmed illusion* spells (spell save DC 20). For every 10-foot section crossed, the traps generate the image of a huge fire elemental. Up to 4 such illusions may be generated in this manner. Thus, a character who crosses 30 feet of the sand pit triggers 3 *programmed illusions* of **fire elementals**.

The staircase in the eastern side of the chamber leads down to the first level. The staircase on the western side leads to the tower's third level.

A staircase around the edge of the room leads to a door on the third floor. It is magically locked and warded, as are all the doors in the tower.

3-A. The Chamber of Illusions

The first task a practitioner of illusions learned from Jhedophar was to tell the difference between illusion and reality. To that end, Jhedophar constructed an illusionary maze on this floor of his tower. Apprentices traced their way through the illusory walls to find the staircase leading up to the tower's fourth floor.

Upon entering the chamber of illusions, 2 **spellgorged zombies**[B] stalk the characters through the maze, ignoring any walls as they are immune to illusions. One of the zombies casts *cloudkill* before closing to slam opponents with its fists. The other casts *confusion* followed by *magic missile*.

Remember to include the effects of the tower's continuous *desecrate*[A] spell on all undead.

3-B. False Staircase

Jhedophar created a partial staircase along the western edge of the chamber of illusions. It extends upward about 20 feet with the rest being a permanent *silent image* of a staircase continuing up to the fourth floor. A character following the illusory stairs is considered

to be interacting with them, so automatically realizes their illusory nature. But the character still must succeed on a DC 15 Dexterity saving throw or fall the 20 feet to the floor below, suffering 2d6 bludgeoning damage. Upon falling, a *weird* spell (spell save DC 20) is cast on the falling victim, causing her to vividly picture herself falling to her death. It lasts only a single round, so the target need only make one Wisdom saving throw. A creature that fails the saving throws takes 22 (4d10) psychic damage.

4. The Chamber of Enchantments

This floor has two rooms.

4-A. Still the Prettiest

This room is filled with mirrors and paintings, tapestries and murals. One mirror is a *mirror of charming*[A]. Since all the mirrors reflect one another, anyone looking into a mirror must succeed on a DC 15 Wisdom saving throw or become infatuated with his or her own image and be unable leave the mirror's presence. Such creatures merely stand transfixed, brushing their hair and reciting such phrases as "Still the prettiest," or "My, but aren't I a fine one?" characters may make an additional DC 15 Wisdom saving throw if anyone tries to pull them away from staring at their image. On a failure, they become enraged and attack their allies. Each such creature may repeat the saving throw at the end of each of its turns while in combat, ending the effect on itself on a success.

The chamber contains various bones and dust-covered equipment of adventurers who starved to death in front of the mirrors. Standing in front of one of the mirrors is a dwarf whose beard has grown so long that it curls upon the floor. He is so covered in dust that he appears to be a marble statue, requiring a character to succeed on a DC 18 Wisdom (Perception) check to notice that he is actually alive.

Imbo the Undying[B] was sent to the Tower of Jhedophar some years ago on behalf of his benefactors to retrieve the *mandrake staff*[A]. While Imbo is a thoroughly evil dwarf, he may assist the characters should they break the enchantment upon him.

If freed, he helps the party up until Jhedophar is destroyed then betrays them at the first opportunity he gets to gain the *mandrake staff* for himself. Of course, in his berserk rage at being pulled away from

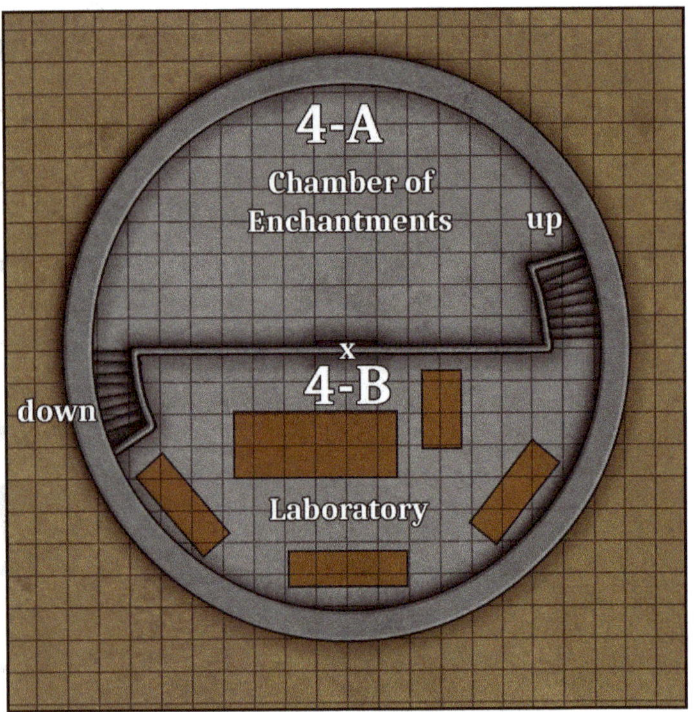

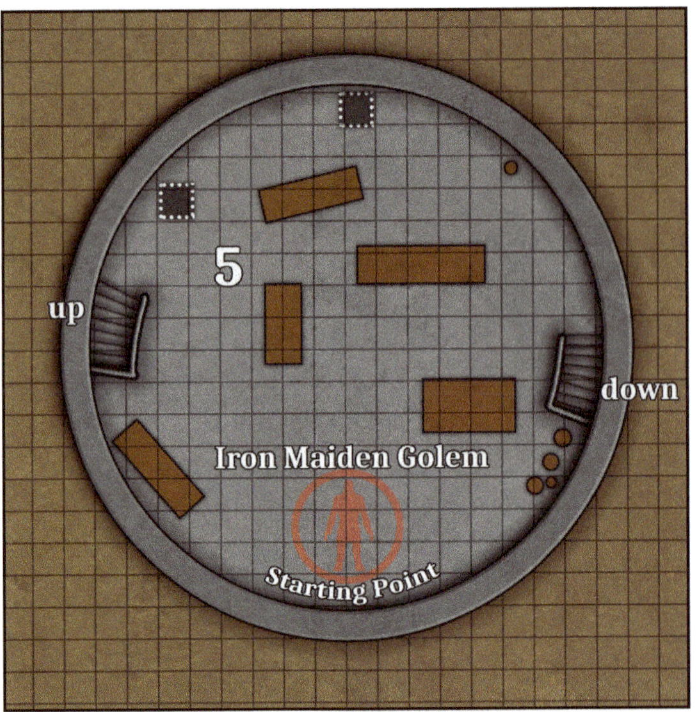

the *mirror of charming*, he may "accidentally" kill someone. If asked how he managed to survive so long without food or water, Imbo points to a pink and green sphere circling his head and explains that it is an *ioun stone of sustenance*. While using it, he says, he didn't need to eat, drink, or sleep. He is lying, and the stone is actually an *ioun stone of leadership*.

Roleplaying Notes. Imbo is as ruthless and bloodthirsty as it gets. Due to a particular curse upon his wretched soul, he cannot truly die, as none of the gods of the heavens or the dukes of Hell will tolerate his despicable presence among them for more than a moment. Even if disintegrated or reduced to ashes by the flames of a dragon, his essence remains and slowly reforms over time. He eventually returns — with slight gaps in his memory — as a stout and cruel dwarf. The reformed Imbo always seeks out the same style of weapons and gear, and always joins up with the cruelest and most powerful of allies. Imbo is an accomplished thief and liar, and takes great pains to conceal his deceptions from the characters until the very last moment when he springs one of his particularly vile traps upon them.

Treasure. A successful DC 20 Wisdom (Perception) check of the bones and rotting equipment uncovers 1d4 random high quality weapons, and 2d100 gp. Jhedophar long ago gathered any magical items or gems from these failed intruders.

4-B. LABORATORY

The second room within the chamber of enchantments is an alchemical laboratory with more than 2000 gp worth of high quality alchemical equipment that reduces the time and expense of brewing each potion created using it by 20%. Several potions and bottles of unguents and reagents are found within this room. It is guarded by an **invisible stalker** that immediately attacks.

Treasure. Also found within this room are a *potion of suggestion*[A], a *potion of glibness*[A], *oil of etherealness*, and a *potion of poison*.

A staircase leads upward to the next floor.

5. THE CHAMBER OF TRANSMUTATION

Jhedophar works out some of the most complicated forms of magic here, changing one object or item into another. The chamber is filled with benches and tables laden with items such as lead coins, small

amounts of gold, rare gems, and the like. Several small cages and a large barred cell are in the corner of the room. The cages contain various creatures such as dire rats and pigeons. Several tools and gears are found in this workshop. If gathered, the tools are of high quality and valued at 1,000 gp.

A **shield guardian** attacks any unbidden intruder entering the chamber of transmutation.

The shield guardian is programmed to trigger a *confusion* spell (spell save DC 20) and then pummel to a pulp anyone attempting to cause it harm. If the shield guardian loses more than 50% of its hit point maximum, it is programmed to flee to Jhedophar's chamber of divination (**Area 8A**).

A wand sits on a table. Beside it is a set of scales with a pile of gold and gems on one side and lead coins serving as a counterweight. *Detect magic* reveals the wand is magical, but it is trapped with a *true polymorph* trap. A successful DC 25 Intelligence (Investigation) reveals that the wand is magically trapped. The trap can be disabled with a *dispel magic, remove curse,* or similar spell. If the wand is touched without disarming the trap, the creature touching it must succeed on a DC 20 Wisdom saving throw or be transformed into a sheep wearing a blue dress. This transformation lasts until dispelled.

The wand is non-magical but detects as magical because of an *arcanist's magic aura* cast upon it to make it appear as if it is a *wand of polymorph*.

A staircase leads upward to a locked door that is the entryway to the sixth floor.

6. CHAMBER OF NECROMANCY

Upon entering this chamber, the characters find themselves face to face with a **vrock demon** flanked by a pair of **spellgorged zombies**[B]. The vrock and zombies attack the party instantly with spells and spell-like abilities before closing in with melee attacks.

Tactics. In the first round of combat, the vrock uses its Stunning Screech ability and the spellgorged zombies unleash their spells. One spellgorged zombie attacks by casting *blight* targeted on a lightly armored opponent, while the second one casts *contagion* (causing blinding sickness) targeted at another lightly armored opponent. Neither spell requires concentration. On the second round, the vrock moves in and uses its Spores ability upon the characters. The spellgorged zombies move to engage enemies. The vrock and the

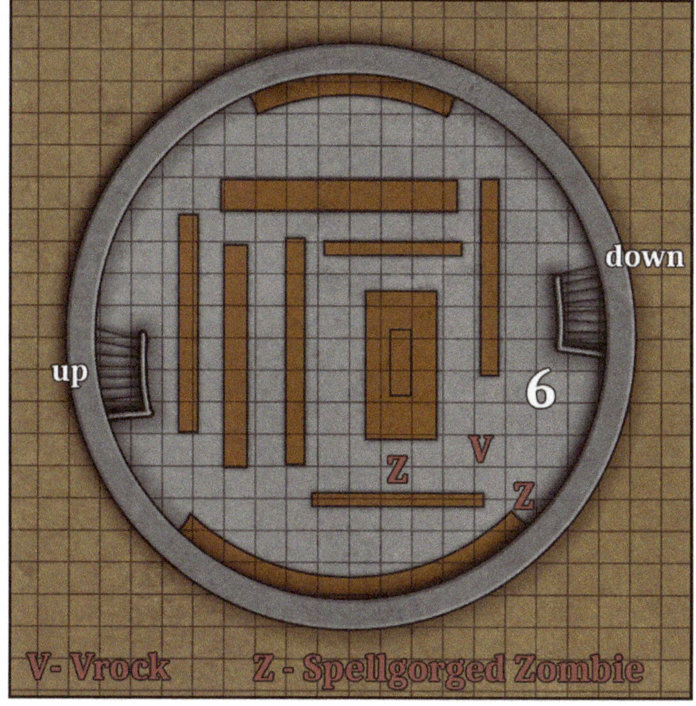

only necromantic spells that offered defensive possibilities and then only to a select and trusted few. All of this changed when Jhedophar dreamed of a beautiful temptress offering him immortality. He pored over his many eldritch tomes and finally sought out eternal life in un-death when he felt age creep into his bones.

Books and scrolls about the necromantic arts and defenses against the powers of the undead line the walls of this chamber, which is more of a library or a study than any other chamber in the tower. A character studying the tomes collected here for weeks of diligent research equal to 6 – the character's Intelligence bonus [minimum of 1 week] gains a permanent +2 bonus to any Intelligence (Arcana) checks concerning undead creatures and spells from the school of necromancy.

Treasure. A character succeeding on a DC 25 Wisdom (Perception) check gleans three *spell scrolls* of value:

Scroll #1. *hold person*, *ray of enfeeblement*, and *gentle repose*
Scroll #2. *vampiric touch* x2 and *blight*
Scroll #3. *arcane hand*, *create undead*, and *animate dead*

7. The Chamber of Conjuration

Binding runes are inscribed on the walls, doors, and floor of this chamber. Only high adepts were allowed entrance to this chamber where Jhedophar conferred with extraplanar forces in his magical research.

Guarding the chamber are 2 **spellgorged zombies**[B] triggered to destroy anyone who enters the chamber unbidden.

Tactics. The first spellgorged zombie casts *cloudkill* while the second summons *black tentacles* near heavily armored characters.

Remember to include the effects of the tower's continuous *desecrate*[A] spell on all undead.

A large magic circle is inscribed on the floor in the center of this chamber. Anyone crossing the threshold of the magical circle triggers a *magic mouth* that utters a curse in Common in Jhedophar's raspy

zombies gang up on one target at a time until destroyed or until they defeat the characters.

Remember to include the effects of the tower's continuous *desecrate*[A] spell on all undead.

In life, Jhedophar was no fan of necromantic magic. However, since becoming a lich, Jhedophar has become a master of all things undead, even raising the bodies of his former apprentices as a new form of undead servant, the spellgorged zombie. Jhedophar taught initiates

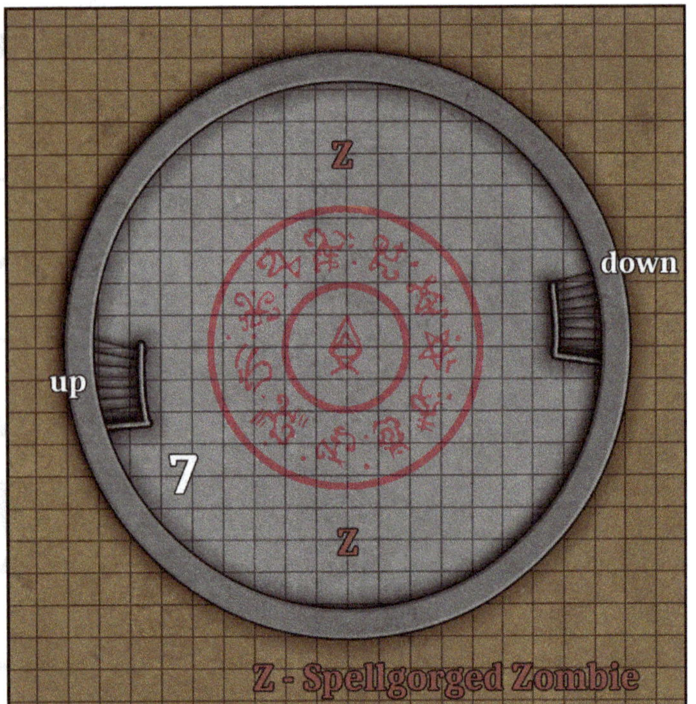

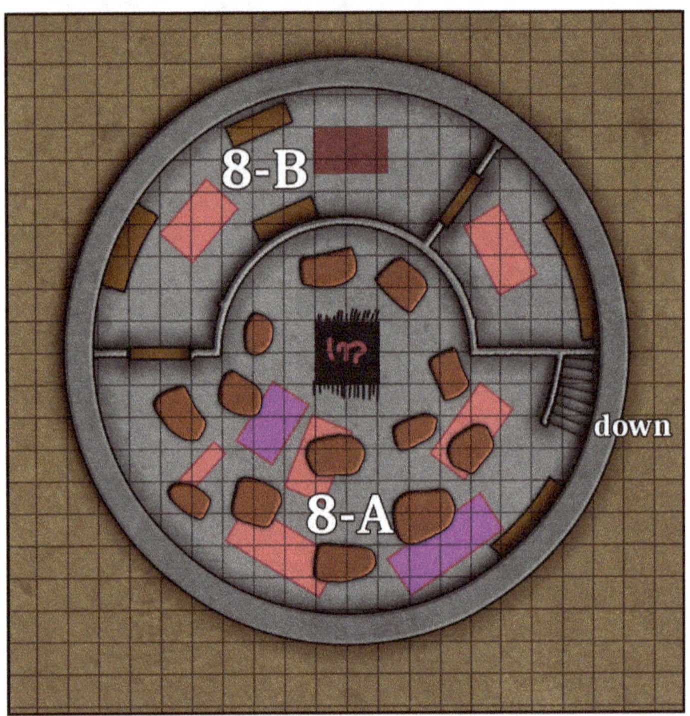

voice: *"Curious of magic, are you? Magic is a force to fear! Your courage fails you in the face of the arcane!"* Any character that can hear the voice and who understands Common must succeed on a DC 20 Wisdom saving throw or be affected by a *mass suggestion* spell which lasts 10 days or until a *remove curse* or similar spell is used. Affected creatures run in terror from anyone or anything perceived to be using arcane magical powers. A character making a successful DC 22 Intelligence (Investigation) check can discover the presence of a magical trap in the pigment of the circle. Before it is triggered, the trap may be neutralized with *dispel magic, remove curse*, or a similar spell.

A staircase leads to the next floor of the tower. A locked and warded door enters the eighth floor.

Treasure. A *brazier of commanding fire elementals* filled with brimstone sits in the center of a magic circle. If Jhedophar is within his chamber of divination (**Area 8**), he can cause the fire to light and summon a **fire elemental**. The elemental throws its support in with the spellgorged zombies.

8-A. The Chamber of Divination

This floor of the tower holds Jhedophar's private quarters. It is also where Jhedophar uses his *crystal ball* to spot troubles around the world and to seek the deeper mysteries of the universe from within and without the realms of existence. This special divination chamber is for Jhedophar alone to use; apprentices were never allowed entry here due to the level of concentration required for deep scrying. The room is filled with soft throw pillows and draped with velvet curtains. Several *gems of seeing* are on the pillows, and a large *crystal ball* sits on a gilt golden pedestal in the center of the room. A door to the north leads to Jhedophar's private quarters. Jhedophar placed a permanent rune of *nondetection* upon the ceiling of this chamber to allow him to scry freely without worrying about being seen by others.

Unless already encountered elsewhere, **Jhedophar**[B] finally reveals himself to the characters when they reach this room. He stands ominously before the characters, his bony hands clasped around the twisted length of the *mandrake staff*[A].

> This lush chamber is filled with plush pillows and shrouded in velvet curtains. Gems gleam from their place on the pillows, and a crystal ball reflects the light. A powerful-looking man stands on the far side of the room, his bony hands clasped around the twisted length of a wooden staff.
>
> *"My name is Jhedophar, and you must be powerful indeed if you seek to steal this twisted staff of root and flesh from me. But think first what you could gain instead if you wait a moment and listen to my parley."*

If characters wait and listen to him, Jhedophar explains that the tower, the staff, and even all the treasures within his tower are worthless compared to his knowledge gained through centuries of researching the occult. In fact, he has grown tired of constantly defending the tower and is arranging to leave it altogether for a new place that is "a bit roomier" with a "more pleasant view."

But, Jhedophar explains, he has no intention of just "giving away" his belongings. He points out that a red dragon named Exeterus is now a squatter in the bowels of the labyrinth. If the characters are brave enough, they may be able to overcome the dragon, in which case he promises to give the tower to the characters. Jhedophar purposely does not mention the *mandrake staff* when he offers to hand over the tower. He has no intention of willingly giving up the staff. However, Jhedophar is very intelligent and understands that a large force of adventurers powerful enough to survive the traps and beasts within his lair may well be able to harm or even slay him.

Beside Jhedophar is a carved statuette of Beluiri sitting on his personal altar to his dark queen. The altar and statuette are hidden beneath a drapery of pure black silk that he keeps over them when entertaining "living" guests. The statuette is enchanted with a *symbol of stunning*, triggered when viewed by any living creature (see Tactics below). The altar of Beluiri is a foul and truly evil set piece to this otherwise lavish chamber. Jhedophar sacrificed each of his apprentices upon this altar and turned them into **spellgorged zombies**[B]. The altar is under the influence of permanent *desecrate*[A] (which benefits Jhedophar) and *hallow* (unholy, 60-foot radius, living creatures who fail their saving throw are vulnerable to fire damage) spells. Jhedophar cannot be turned while in its presence.

If characters attack (or if they reject his request), he targets the characters with as many deadly spells as possible from his extensive repertoire before casting *plane shift* and making his way to his new fortress upon the Plane of Molten Skies. He plans to work as an ambassador and spy for his dread Queen Beluiri.

Tactics. Jhedophar has had plenty of time to prepare for the characters and already cast several defensive spells by the time the characters enter the divination chamber. Specifically, he has cast *mage armor*, *mirror image* and *contingency* (if he is reduced to 25% of his maximum hit points or less, *dimension door* will transport him to a safe location where he can *plane shift* to the Plane of Molten Skies). Rather than destroy the chamber, Jhedophar first casts *mass suggestion* to once again try to get all the characters to sit down on the floor and listen to him. If any still fail to hear him out, he sees no recourse but to destroy them and uses a free action to remove the cover from the altar, unleashing the *symbol of stunning*. He then casts *time stop* and takes the following actions while it is effect. On his first turn, he casts *delayed blast fireball*, targeting a point that will encompass the greatest number of characters but not himself. This should not interfere with the *time stop* as he has not affected another creature…yet. He maintains concentration on the *delayed blast fireball* as long as the *time stop* lasts, augmenting its damage each turn. He deliberately ceases concentration and allows the spell to detonate as soon as time begins flowing normally again for the rest of the world. If he has turns to spare during his *time stop*, he will use the *mandrake staff*'s Walk of the Mandrake ability (instructing it to use its Withering and other attacks on a lightly armored character as soon as *time stop* ends), recast *mirror image* to extend its duration, and use a *spell scroll* to cast *disintegrate* on a 20-foot square section of the tower floor under characters' feet. When *time stop* ends, the *delayed blast fireball* goes off, and anyone standing on the disintegrated floor falls 20' to the seventh level of the tower. Jhedophar then attempts to cast *wall of force* to isolate himself from any remaining physical threats. He attempts to to keep characters at bay, dropping them and pelting the characters with offensive spells, including *meteor swarm* from a *spell scroll*.

If the characters severely injure Jhedophar, he *dimension doors* away automatically via his *contingency* spell, recalls the *mandrake staff*[A] to his hand, and *plane shifts* out of the tower to his new fortress in the Plane of Molten Skies — unless prevented by magical means such as an *antimagic field*.

Note. At your discretion, Lartugi may step in to assist the characters if he was not slain previously. Alternately, if the characters are having too easy of a time with Jhedophar, Lartugi could join the fray as a wild card. If Lartugi still lives and Imbo is with the characters, Imbo switches sides, and he and Lartugi fight Jhedophar and the characters to gain the staff.

Consequences. If Jhedophar escapes, the characters might find themselves in a predicament if they previously made a deal with Exeterus. The red dragon most certainly expects the characters to return the *mandrake staff* to him or to be destroyed trying. They must either kill the dragon, or chase Jhedophar through the planes of existence, destroy him, and retrieve the staff lest Exeterus stalk them for the rest of their lives.

Treasure. 6 *gems of seeing* and a *crystal ball of mind reading*. The golden pedestal on which the crystal ball sits is worth 1,390 gp.

Note. The *gems of seeing* work perfectly for Jhedophar should he choose to cast *magic jar* or *imprisonment*.

8-B. JHEDOPHAR'S PRIVATE CHAMBER

Jhedophar's bedchamber contains a writing table with enough ink to scribe 20 levels worth of pages in spellbooks or 40 *spell scrolls*. Enough material spell components are in vials and jars here to cast each spell in his spellbooks six times. A locked secret door is behind an illusory wall. The illusory wall can be seen for what it is with a successful DC 20 Intelligence (Investigation) check. The door is guarded by a *glyph of warding* which produces the explosive runes effect (7th level spell slot) and a falling block trap. The glyph's subtle lines may be detected by a successful DC 20 Intelligence (Investigation) check, and the trap's hair-trigger spring mechanism may be located with a separate successful DC 20 Intelligence (Investigation) check. Only a successful *dispel magic* or similar spell (spell DC 20) removes the glyph. But a character using thieves' tools and succeeding on a DC

18 Dexterity check can neutralize the falling block trap. Both traps are triggered by touching the door in any way. Any creature in a 20 foot wide by 10 foot deep area in front of the door must succeed on a DC 20 Dexterity saving throw or take 35 (10d6) bludgeoning damage from the massive stone.

A small chamber beyond the trapped door holds a staff, several robes, and a bookshelf that contains many different dusty volumes. Scroll cases line the top of the shelves, and a silver dagger hangs from a chain upon a hook.

A character making a successful DC 23 Wisdom (Perception) check discovers an invisible bookshelf that contains Jhedophar's actual spellbooks. The other books are each enchanted with *arcanist's magic aura* to appear magical and trapped with a *ward of* pain. The ward on a particular book can be detected with a successful DC 20 Intelligence (Investigation) check but can only be neutralized with the use of *dispel magic* or similar spell. They are filled with confusing gibberish; Jhedophar cast *illusory script* on them to fool common thieves into thinking they are of great value. They merely confuse a spellcaster attempting to read them as if they were under the effects of a *confusion* spell (spell save DC 20).

Treasure. Jhedophar's spellbooks. These large volumes are covered in *illusory script*. Perusing them gives the impression that they are blank. Characters also find a solid silver *+2 dagger*, a **flying staff**[B] which attacks when touched, a *spell wand*[A] of *sleep*, a *ring of protection*, and 10 *potions of poison*.

Jhedophar keeps spare copies of his spellbooks and his phylactery hidden within a magical chest hidden on the Ethereal Plane using a *secret chest* spell.

CONCLUDING THE ADVENTURE

If the characters made a deal with Exeterus and wrested the *mandrake staff*[A] from Jhedophar, they must still return to face the red dragon. They could also try sneaking off with the goods. If the characters did not make a deal with Exeterus, the dragon notices the commotion from the tower and may be lying in wait for the characters when they attempt to leave. It happily extorts any treasure it can get from them as it decides whether to roast and eat them or to let them go.

The adventure concludes when the characters chase off or destroy Jhedophar and Exeterus. It is hoped they made it out with their lives and some new magic items and treasure. This adventure is not about completing some grand quest or accomplishing some great deed. It is about facing down danger and testing one's mettle against dangerous and deadly foes.

EXTENDING THE ADVENTURE

Exeterus and Jhedophar are great continuing foes you could use in your ongoing campaign. Perhaps the characters decide to hunt down Jhedophar in the Plane of Molten Skies, or they find themselves stalked by the greedy dragon who uses innocent villagers as hostages as he burns and destroys all in his path to find the characters. This offers various roleplaying opportunities as the heroes are soon regarded as harbingers of doom. The story of villages being destroyed in their passing is passed along on the lips of bards and skalds until the characters finally face up to the threat of Exeterus following them.

Jhedophar might also find the characters an amusing challenge and decide to torment them by popping into their lives from time to time. He might also use the characters to secretly do his dirty work. Jhedophar is extremely intelligent and quite selfishly despicable and unpredictable. Evil or neutral characters may find Jhedophar to be a mentor or powerful patron to their dastardly deeds. Above all, Jhedophar is a survivor and seeks to stay that way.

Characters might also try to uncover the many secrets of the fantastic sword *Karelis*[A]. The weapon seeks a strong hero who may finally free her body from imprisonment on the Plane of Agony.

Appendix A: New Magic

This chapter details new spells and magic items found in the adventure.

New Spells

Desecrate

2nd-level necromancy
Casting Time: 1 action
Range: 60 feet
Components: V, S, M (25gp of silver dust)
Duration: 8 hours

Any undead creature within a 20 ft. sphere centered on a point you choose within range gains several benefits due to an influx of negative energy into the area. Each undead's maximum hit points and current hit points increase by 5. Whenever an undead target makes an attack roll, damage roll, or a saving throw, the undead can roll a d4 and add the number rolled to the attack roll, damage roll, or saving throw. Finally, the DC of any saving throw required by a Life Drain ability of an undead is increased by 2. All of these benefits cease for a target when the duration ends or when that target leaves the area of effect. It regains the benefits if it reenters the area of effect.

Ward of Pain

2nd-level abjuration
Casting Time: 1 action
Range: Touch
Components: V, S, M (needle stuck through caster's hand)
Duration: Until dispelled or triggered

Long lost in the annals of time, this spell was purportedly a favorite of the torture mages of Kal Kesh in the dark morning of the world.

Upon casting *ward of pain*, you impart every ounce of agony and torture you can muster upon the object the ward is scribed upon. A creature triggering the ward by touching this object must succeed on a Constitution saving throw or take 5d4 points of force damage. If this damage reduces the target to 0 hit points, the target is unconscious and stable. The material component for this spell is a needle driven through your hand to absorb your inner agony.

At Higher Levels. When you cast this spell using a spell slot of 3rd level or higher, the damage increases by 1d4 for each slot level above 2nd.

Magic Items

Adherer Oil

Potion, rare

This milky glue-like substance is very sticky. It is the alchemically distilled secretion of an adherer. When applied to a creature's body, it causes the blows of enemies' weapons to stick to its body unless its attacker is using a stone weapon or succeeds on a DC 20 Dexterity saving throw. Likewise, individuals coated in *adherer oil* gain a +5 bonus to any grappling checks they make while thus coated. One application of *adherer oil* lasts for 3d6 minutes.

Eyes of Petrification

Wondrous item, very rare

This set of crystal spectacles has 3 charges. As an action, you can expend 1 charge to cast *flesh to stone* on a creature you can see within 30 feet of you.

The eyes regain 1d3 expended charges daily at dawn.

Golden Circlet of Skeleton Warrior Control

The transformation into a skeleton warrior traps the person's soul in a golden circlet. Anyone possessing one of these circlets may exert control over the skeleton warrior (whose soul is trapped therein).

In order to establish or maintain control, the controller must be within 300 feet of the skeleton warrior and must wear the circlet on his head and spend one full round concentrating on the skeleton warrior. If the controller is interrupted during this time, he must succeed on a DC 20 Concentration check to establish control. If the check fails, the controller can try again. While wearing the circlet, the controller cannot wear any other item on his head. Doing so causes the circlet to cease functioning until the other headgear is removed. (A skeleton warrior can still detect the location of its circlet even if the controller wears something on his head to nullify the circlet's powers.)

While wearing the circlet and within 300 feet of the skeleton warrior, the controller can see through the skeleton warrior's eyes and force it to act (attack, search, and so forth). This is called "active" mode. While the skeleton warrior is in active mode, the controller himself cannot take any other action.

Alternately, the controller can place the skeleton warrior in "passive" mode. In this mode, the skeleton warrior stands motionless and inert. The controller cannot see through the skeleton warrior's eyes but he himself is free to act. If the controller moves more than 300 feet away from the skeleton warrior or if the circlet is removed from the controller's head, the skeleton warrior automatically enters passive mode.

The controller can switch the skeleton warrior between active and passive mode as a bonus action. Should the controller ever lose the circlet (through accident, theft, or simply by discarding it), the skeleton warrior instantly stops what it is doing and moves as quickly as possible toward the former controller and attempts to destroy him or her. If a skeleton warrior ever gains control of the circlet that contains its soul, it places the circlet on its head and "dies", vanishing in a flash of light. The circlet falls to the ground and crumbles to dust.

Karelis

Weapon (sword), legendary (requires attunement by a creature of good alignment)

This adamantine longsword is of magnificent craftsmanship, having a suppleness not normally seen in such a weapon. Its chiseled and engraved hilt is done in the ancient elven style of sword dancers, with a green dragon skin wrist thong attached to its star sapphire pommel stone. The emeralds adorning the cross hilt are embedded to appear like a pair of almond-shaped eyes of deep beauty and sadness.

You gain a +3 bonus to attack and damage rolls made with this magic weapon. In addition, it has the following additional properties.

Sentience. Karelis is a sentient neutral good weapon with an Intelligence of 18, Wisdom of 14, and Charisma of 20. She has hearing and darkvision out to a range of 120 feet.

The weapon can speak, read, and understand Abyssal, Celestial, Common, Elven, Infernal, and the secret tongue of the n'gathau[B]. She can also communicate telepathically with her wielder.

Karelis' special purpose is to destroy the horrid thing her body has become. Although her soul is trapped within the magical blade, Karelis' body lives on in the Plane of Agony. It is now a horrid, twisted, tortured being called a n'gathau. Neither the soul of Karelis nor Lord Tork are certain of the truth, but they suspect that Jhedophar sold Karelis to demonic creatures called the n'gathau in exchange for vile wisdom and great power. *Karelis* does not know the new name the n'gathau bequeathed to her body, nor does she even know what her body looks like after being twisted and tortured and reshaped by the ghastly rulers of the Plane of Agony. The sword's purpose is to lead heroes appropriate to the task to the Plane of Agony to destroy the n'gathau that Karelis has become, thus allowing her soul to escape the blade and go on to her eternal reward.

While on the Material Plane, her will is to destroy any n'gathau and their minions that she or her wielder meets.

Truthseeker. Karelis has Insight +10 and will use this skill to inform her wielder of any deception or nefarious intent of those with whom her wielder interacts. The wielder may also cast the following spells:

At will: *detect magic*.

3/day: *detect evil and good*

1/day: *lesser globe of invulnerability*

Deathwatch Dance. Whenever the bearer of *Karelis* drops below 0 hp, *Karelis* animates as a *dancing sword* to defend the fallen hero for 4 rounds. When this effect takes place, the ghostly image of the elf-maiden *Karelis* appears before the sword bearer's enemies and allies alike as she defends his fallen form, although the wounded and unconscious hero may never see this magnificent sight. Should the hero be healed while *Karelis* defends his form, the blade drops to within reach of the hero so that he may again grasp her hilt and rejoin the fight. Her image vanishes upon his return to consciousness.

Song of Karelis. Twice per day, *Karelis* may be asked to sing her song of battle. This song acts similar to the Bardic inspiration ability and grants the bearer and his allies within 30 feet each a d10 inspiration die. The lilting elven war-song causes the blade to appear to vibrate, the notes resounding in a 30-foot-wide radius around the bearer of the blade.

Bane of N'gathau. When combating a n'gathau, the wielder of *Karelis* is granted a +3 bonus to all saving throws and a +3 bonus to AC.

MANDRAKE STAFF

Staff, legendary (requires attunement by a spellcaster)

This staff is roughly 6 feet long and nearly 3 inches thick. It is dark and twisted, having the vague appearance of a tortured, withered man. The top of the staff looks like the screaming head of a damned spirit. Legends abound as to the true source of the staff. Whispers and myths speak of a great mandrake root as strong as darkwood dug from beneath the feet of a hanged murderer. It was given life and imbued with magical power by the witches of the Stench-Hollow Downs. Others claim the staff's power is much older. The staff possesses many astounding and deadly qualities and has been sought after by masters of the school of transmutation for its powers of strengthening their magic twofold.

You gain a +3 bonus to attack and damage rolls made with this magic weapon. In addition, it has the following additional properties.

Withering (2/week). A successful melee attack with this staff against creatures of up to Large size causes a portion of the body so touched to wither away unless a successful DC 22 Constitution saving throw is made. On a failed save, a strike to a limb causes that limb to drop off, a strike to the head results in instant death, and a strike to the torso reduces the target's Constitution score by 2d6 points. The target dies if this reduces its Constitution to 0. Lost limbs and Constitution points may be recovered only with a wish or regenerate spell. In the event of death, only true resurrection may raise the victim. Determine where the withering strike lands by rolling 1d6: 1—head; 2—right arm; 3—left arm; 4—right leg; 5—left leg; 6—torso.

Poison (1/day). A target struck with the mandrake staff when this ability is activated must succeed on a DC 20 Constitution saving throw or become poisoned, take 5 (1d10) poison damage, and subtract an amount equal to the poison damage taken from its maximum hit points. Only arcane spellcasters such as sorcerers, warlocks, and wizards may use this feature.

Empowered Transmutation. Whenever you cast a transmutation spell while holding the staff, the spell save DC for that spell is 1 higher than normal.

Spells. You may use the staff to cast one of the following spells, requiring no material components:

3/day: *blink*

2/day: *passwall*

1/day: *flesh to stone, etherealness, plane shift*

Walk of the Mandrake. Once per week, the staff may be commanded to animate and walk about on its own accord for up to 1 hour. The staff sprouts a pair of root-like legs that allow it a movement rate of 30 feet. The staff has an Armor Class of 20, 32 hit points, and attacks with your proficiency bonus. While the staff is moving independently of its master, it may use any of its special abilities as long as those special abilities have not gone beyond their allocated number of uses. You may use a bonus action to end this function and return the staff immediately to your hand.

MIRROR OF CHARMING

Wondrous item, very rare

This ornate polished silver mirror is bordered in an intricately worked golden frame that makes it appear much like a boudoir mirror. It is roughly 5 feet tall by 3 feet wide and affords anyone gazing into it a nearly full-length view of themselves. Upon gazing into the mirror, the viewer must succeed on a DC 20 Wisdom saving throw or become enraptured by its own appearance, unable to stop looking at itself. Removing a viewer from gazing into the mirror causes the viewer to make a second DC 20 Wisdom saving throw. On a failure, the viewer becomes enraged for 1d6 rounds, attacking anyone who disturbs the viewing. On a success, the effect is ended on that creature. Each affected creature may repeat this saving throw at the end of each round of combat, ending the effect on itself on a success. Once a creature has succeeded on a saving throw against the mirror's effects, that creature is immune to those effects for 24 hours.

POTION OF GLIBNESS

Potion, uncommon

For 1 hour after you drink this clear, light purple potion, you gain a +3 bonus to all Charisma (Deception or Persuasion) checks.

POTION OF SUGGESTION

Potion, rare

Within 1 hour of drinking this thick chalky potion, you may cast the spell *suggestion* (spell save DC 13) once without the need for material components.

RING OF PROTECTION

Wondrous item, rarity varies (requires attunement)

While wearing this ring, you gain a bonus to your AC and saving throws. The amount of the bonus depends on the ring's rarity.

Ring of...	Rarity	Bonus
Protection	rare	+1
Greater protection	very rare	+2
Superior protection	legendary	+3

RING OF WIZARDRY, CURSED

Ring, very rare (requires attunement by a sorcerer, warlock, or wizard)

While wearing this cursed ring, you believe your number of spell slots for a randomly determined spell level that you can cast is twice as great as it really is. When you "cast" a spell slot that you do not truly have, you alone perceive a harmless, illusionary version of the desired spell effect.

Scroll Case of Obscuring

Wondrous item, rare

You may store up to five scrolls of any kind within this innocuous looking scroll case's ebon-wood compartment. The scroll case is continually under the effects of a *nondetection* spell. Also, it does not radiate magic for purposes of a *detect magic* spell, regardless of its contents. So would-be thieves using scrying devices and magic will be more likely to ignore the scroll case's presence.

Suzette

Weapon (battleaxe), legendary (requires attunement by a creature of evil alignment)

You gain a +3 bonus to attack and damage rolls made with this magic weapon. It has the following additional properties:

Sentience. Suzette is a sentient lawful evil weapon with an Intelligence of 9, Wisdom of 6, and Charisma of 18. It has hearing and darkvision out to 120 feet. The weapon communicates telepathically with its owner and speaks Common and Infernal. Suzette craves destruction and encourages its owner to kill any and all potential targets who do not submit.

Cleaving. Once per turn, if you hit a target with this weapon, you may make one additional attack with this weapon on a different target within your reach.

Devilish. You gain a +2 bonus to damage rolls made with this magic weapon against celestials and fey.

Spell Wand

Wand, varies (requires attunement by a spellcaster)

A spell wand allows you to cast a single spell without material components. While holding it, you can use an action to expend 1 charge to cast the spell associated with the wand. You must be able to speak the command and point the wand at the target. If the spell has a range of touch, then you must touch the target with the wand, although you still use the wand's spell attack bonus to attempt the touch. In general, the wand casts the spell with the lowest possible spell slot. The rarity, save DC, spell attack modifier, number of charges, and charge refresh per 24 hours are shown below, depending on the level of spell stored in the wand.

Spell Wand Table

Spell Level	Rarity	Save DC	Attack Bonus	Charges	Charge Refresh
Cantrip	Common	13	+5	10	1d6 + 4
1st	Uncommon	13	+5	10	1d6 + 4
2nd	Uncommon	13	+5	7	1d6 + 1
3rd	Rare	15	+7	7	1d6 + 1
4th	Rare	15	+7	7	1d6 + 1
5th	Very Rare	17	+9	4	1d3 + 1
6th	Very Rare	17	+9	4	1d3 + 1
7th	Very Rare	18	+10	3	1d3
8th	Legendary	18	+10	3	1d3
9th	Legendary	19	+11	3	1d3

Appendix B: New Monsters

Barrow Wight

Medium undead, chaotic evil

Armor Class 14 (studded leather)
Hit Points 45 (6d8 + 18)
Speed 30 ft.

STR	DEX	CON	INT	WIS	CHA
16 (+3)	14 (+2)	16 (+3)	10 (+0)	13 (+1)	15 (+2)

Skills Perception +3, Stealth +4
Damage resistances necrotic; bludgeoning, piercing and slashing from nonmagical weapons that are not silvered
Damage immunities poison
Condition immunities exhaustion, poisoned
Senses darkvision 60 ft., passive Perception 13
Languages the language it knew in life
Challenge 3 (700 XP)

Gaze of Insanity. If a creature starts its turn within 30 feet of the barrow wight and the two of them can see each other, the barrow wight can force the creature to make a DC 13 Wisdom saving throw if the barrow wight is not incapacitated. On a failed save, the creature is affected by a short-term madness effect for 1 minute. Determine the effect from the table below.

d100	Effect (lasts 1 minute)
01–20	The target retreats into its mind and becomes paralyzed. The effect ends if the creature takes any damage.
21–30	The creature is incapacitated, and can only scream, laugh, or weep hysterically.
31–40	The creature is frightened and must use its actions to flee from the source of its fear.
41–50	The creature babbles incoherently and cannot speak normally or cast spells.
51–60	The creature must use its action to attack the nearest creature.
61–70	The creature hallucinates vividly, incurring disadvantage on all ability checks.
71–75	The creature does whatever anyone tells it to do that isn't obviously self-destructive.
76–80	The creature experiences an overpowering urge to eat something strange, such as dirt, offal, or slime.
81–90	The creature is stunned.
91–00	The creature falls unconscious.

The target can repeat the saving throw at the end of each of its turns. A successful save ends the effect and renders the target immune to the same barrow wight's insanity gaze for 24 hours.

A creature that isn't surprised can avert its eyes to avoid the saving throw at the start of its turn. If the creature does so, it can't see the barrow wight until the start of its next turn, when it can avert its eyes again. If the creature looks at the barrow wight in the meantime, it must immediately make the save.

Sunlight Sensitivity. While in sunlight, the wight has disadvantage on attack rolls, as well as on Wisdom (Perception) checks that rely on sight.

Actions

Slam. *Melee weapon attack:* +5 to hit, reach 5 ft., one creature. *Hit:* 6 (1d6+3) bludgeoning damage plus 6 (1d6 + 3) necrotic damage. The target must succeed on a DC 13 Constitution saving throw or its hit point maximum is reduced by an amount equal to the necrotic damage taken. This reduction lasts until the target takes a long rest. The target dies if this effect reduces its hit point maximum to zero.

A humanoid slain by this attack rises 1d4 rounds later as a barrow wight under the control of the wight that killed it unless the humanoid is restored to life or its body is destroyed. The wight can have no more than three barrow wights under its control at one time.

Bloody Bones

Medium undead, chaotic evil

Armor Class 15 (natural armor)
Hit Points 60 (8d8 + 24)
Speed 30 ft.

STR	DEX	CON	INT	WIS	CHA
16 (+3)	16 (+3)	17 (+3)	10 (+0)	12 (+1)	5 (−3)

Skills Perception +4, Stealth +6
Damage Resistances fire
Damage Immunities poison
Senses darkvision 60 ft., passive Perception 14
Languages understands all language it knew in life but can't speak
Challenge 5 (1,800 XP)

Slippery. The bloody bones is coated in bloody mucus and has advantage on any Dexterity (Acrobatics) checks it makes to avoid being grappled.
Expendable Tendrils. Each of the bloody bones' tendrils can be attacked (AC 18; 10 hit points; immunity to psychic damage). Destroying a tendril deals no damage to the bloody bones, which can regrow a replacement tendril in one hour.
Rend. If the bloody bones hits the same target with both of its Claw attacks, it deals an additional 10 (2d6 +3) slashing damage to that target.

Actions

Multiattack. The bloody bones makes four Tendril attacks, uses Reel, and makes two Claw attacks.
Tendril. *Melee Weapon Attack:* +6 to hit, reach 30 ft., one creature. *Hit:* 5 (1d4 + 3) slashing damage and the target is grappled (escape DC 16). Until the grapple ends, the target is restrained and has disadvantage on Strength checks and Strength saving throws, and the bloody bones can't use the same tendril on another target.
Claw. *Melee Weapon Attack:* +6 to hit, reach 5 ft., one target. *Hit:* 7 (1d8 + 3) slashing damage.
Reel. The bloody bones pulls each creature grappled by it up to 25 feet straight toward it.

Crypt Thing

Medium undead, neutral

Armor Class 15 (natural armor)
Hit Points 84 (13d8 + 26)
Speed 30 ft.

STR	DEX	CON	INT	WIS	CHA
12 (+1)	16 (+3)	15 (+2)	12 (+1)	14 (+2)	16 (+3)

Skills Deception +6, Perception +5
Senses darkvision 60 ft., passive Perception 15
Languages Common
Challenge 7 (2,900 XP)

Magic Weapons. The crypt thing's weapon attacks are magical.

Actions

Multiattack. The crypt thing makes two attacks with its Claws.

Claws. Melee Weapon Attack: +6 to hit, reach 5 ft., one target. *Hit:* 13 (3d6 + 3) slashing damage and 10 (3d6) necrotic damage.

Teleport Other **(1/day).** As an action, the crypt thing can teleport all creatures within 50 feet of it to a randomly determined location. A creature affected by the crypt thing's Teleport Other must make a DC 15 Wisdom saving throw to avoid being teleported.

An affected creature is teleported in a random direction and a random distance (1d10 x 100 feet) away from the crypt thing. Roll randomly for each creature that fails its saving throw.

If the affected creature would arrive in a place already occupied by an object or another creature, the affected creature takes 14 (4d6) force damage and is not teleported.

Demiurge

Medium undead, chaotic evil

Armor Class 17
Hit Points 90 (12d8 + 36)
Speed 30 ft., fly 40 ft.

STR	DEX	CON	INT	WIS	CHA
6 (–2)	16 (+3)	16 (+3)	14 (+2)	14 (+2)	18 (+4)

Saving Throws Dex +7, Wis +6
Skills Insight +6, Stealth +7
Damage Resistances cold, fire, lightning, thunder
Damage Immunities acid, necrotic, poison; bludgeoning, piercing, and slashing from nonmagical attacks that aren't cold iron
Condition Immunities charmed, exhaustion, frightened, grappled, paralyzed, petrified, poisoned, prone, restrained
Senses darkvision 60 ft., passive Perception 12
Languages the languages it knew in life
Challenge 9 (5,000 XP)

Incorporeal Movement. The demiurge can move through other creatures and objects as if they were difficult terrain. It takes 5 (1d10) force damage if it ends its turn inside an object.

Transfixing Gaze. If a creature starts its turn within 30 feet of the demiurge and the two of them can see each other, the demiurge can force the creature to make a DC 16 Wisdom saving throw if the demiurge isn't incapacitated. On a failed save, the creature is paralyzed for 1 minute. It may repeat the saving throw at the end of each of its turns, ending the effect on itself on a success.

A creature that isn't surprised can avert its eyes to avoid the saving throw at the start of its turn. If it does so, it can't see the demiurge until the start of its next turn, when it can avert its eyes again. If it looks at the demiurge in the meantime, it must immediately make the save.

Unnatural Aura. Both wild and domesticated animals can sense the unnatural presence of a demiurge at a distance of 30 feet. They will not willingly approach nearer than that and panic if forced to do so; they remain panicked as long as they are within that range.

Actions

Multiattack. The demiurge makes two Touch attacks.

Touch. Melee Weapon Attack: +7 to hit, reach 5 ft., one target. *Hit:* 10 (2d6 + 3) necrotic damage.

Soul Touch. The demiurge chooses a creature in its space. That creature must make a DC 16 Charisma saving throw. On a failure, the creature's hit points are reduced to 0 and it is rendered unconscious. On a success, the creature is immune to the demiurge's Soul Touch for 24 hours.

Exeterus

Exeterus is a standard adult red dragon with the following changes and additions:

Challenge 18 (20,000 XP)

Spellcasting. Exeterus is an 9th-level spellcaster. His spellcasting ability is Charisma (spell save DC 19 , +11 to hit with spell attacks). Exeterus has the following spells prepared:

Cantrips (at will): *dancing lights, light, mage hand, minor illusion, prestidigitation*
1st level (4 slots): *burning hands, charm person, shield, silent image*
2nd level (3 slots): *invisibility, shatter, web*
3rd level (3 slots): *counterspell, dispel magic, slow*
4th level (2 slots): *dimension door, wall of fire*
5th level (1 slot): *scrying*

Heightened Spell **(3/day).** When he casts a spell that forces a creature to make a saving throw to resist its effects, Exeterus can give one target disadvantage on its first saving throw made against the spell.

Flying Staff

This staff is identical to an **animated object: flying sword** except for the following changes:

False Appearance: While the staff remains motionless and isn't flying, it is indistinguishable from a normal staff.

Staff. Melee weapon attack: +3 to hit, reach 5 ft., one target. *Hit:* 5 (1d8 + 1) bludgeoning damage.

Grytis

Medium monstrosity, chaotic evil

Armor Class 17 (natural armor)
Hit Points 119 (14d8 + 56)

Speed 30 ft., fly 60 ft.

STR	DEX	CON	INT	WIS	CHA
18 (+4)	16 (+3)	19 (+4)	8 (−1)	10 (+0)	7 (−2)

Skills Stealth +6
Damage Resistances bludgeoning, piercing, and slashing from nonmagical attacks that aren't adamantine
Damage Immunities poison
Condition Immunities exhaustion, petrified, poisoned
Senses darkvision 60 ft., passive Perception 10
Languages Common, Terran
Challenge 6 (2,300 XP)

False Appearance. While Grytis sits motionless, it is indistinguishable from natural stone and can't be detected as alive by any means.

Actions

Multiattack. Grytis makes one Bite attack and two with its Claws; it can Gore once with its horns instead of using its Bite.

Bite. *Melee Weapon Attack:* +7 to hit, reach 5 ft., one target. *Hit:* 11 (2d6 + 4) piercing damage.

Claw. *Melee Weapon Attack:* +7 to hit, reach 5 ft., one target. *Hit:* 13 (2d8 + 4) slashing damage.

Gore. *Melee Weapon Attack:* +7 to hit, reach 5 ft., one target. *Hit:* 11 (2d6 + 4) piercing damage.

IMBO THE UNDYING

Medium humanoid (dwarf), chaotic evil

Armor Class 20 (*+1 adamantine breastplate*, shield)
Hit Points 127 (15d8 + 60)
Speed 40 ft.

STR	DEX	CON	INT	WIS	CHA
19 (+4)	15 (+2)	18 (+4)	16 (+3)	16 (+3)	15 (+2)

Saving Throws Str +8, Dex +6, Con +8, Int +7
Skills Acrobatics +10, Athletics +8, Deception +10, Perception +11, Sleight of Hand +6, Stealth +10
Senses passive Perception 21
Languages Common, Dwarvish, thieves' cant
Challenge 11 (7,200 XP)

***Action Surge* (recharges after a short or long rest).** On his turn, Imbo the Undying can take one additional action on top of his regular action and a possible bonus action.

Cunning Action. Imbo the Undying can take a bonus action on each of his turns in combat. The action can only be used to take the following actions: Dash, Disengage, Hide, Use an Object, make a Dexterity (Sleight of Hand) check, or use thieves' tools to disarm a trap or open a lock,

Defense. While Imbo the Undying is wearing armor, he gains a +1 bonus to AC (included above).

Evasion. When Imbo the Undying is subjected to an effect that allows him to make a Dexterity saving throw to take only half damage, he instead takes no damage if he succeeds on the saving throw, and only half damage if he fails.

Immune to Critical Hits. All critical hits against Imbo the Undying become normal hits because of his adamantine breastplate.

Reckless Attack. When Imbo the Undying makes his first attack on his turn, he can decide to attack recklessly. Doing so gives him advantage on melee weapon attack rolls using Strength during this turn, but attack rolls against him have advantage until his next turn.

Sneak Attack. Once per turn, Imbo the Undying deals an extra 4d6 damage to one creature he hits with an attack if he has advantage on the attack roll. He does not need advantage on the attack roll if another enemy of the target is within 5 feet of it, that enemy isn't incapacitated, and Imbo the Undying does not have disadvantage on the attack roll.

Special Equipment. Imbo the Undying possesses *gauntlets of ogre power*, *boots of speed*, and an *ioun stone of leadership*.

Uncanny Dodge. When an attacker that he can see hits Imbo the Undying with an attack, he can use his reaction to halve the attack's damage against him.

Actions

Multiattack. Imbo the Undying makes two weapon attacks.

+2 Dwarven Thrower. *Melee or Ranged Weapon Attack:* +10 to hit, reach 5 ft. or range 20/60 ft., one target. *Hit:* 10 (1d8 + 6) bludgeoning damage or 15 (2d8 + 6) bludgeoning damage if thrown. The hammer returns to Imbo's hand immediately after a thrown attack.

+1 Battleaxe. *Melee Weapon Attack:* +9 to hit, reach 5 ft., one target. *Hit:* 9 (1d8 + 5) slashing damage.

Bonus Actions

***Rage* (4/day).** Imbo the Undying can enter a rage. While raging, he has advantage on Strength checks and Strength saving throws. When he makes a melee weapon attack using Strength, he gains a +2 bonus to the damage roll. He has resistance to bludgeoning, piercing, and slashing damage. This rage lasts for 1 minute. It ends early if Imbo the Undying is knocked unconscious or if his turn ends and he hasn't attacked a hostile creature since his last turn or taken damage since then. He can also end his rage on his turn as a bonus action.

***Second Wind* (recharges after a short or long rest).** Imbo the Undying regains 1d10 + 2 hit points.

JHEDOPHAR

Jhedophar is a standard lich with a Constitution of 18 and the following changes and additions:

Armor Class 21 (*bracers of defense, greater ring of protection,* and *mage armor*)
Hit Points 153 (18d8 + 72)
Challenge 22 (41,000 XP)

Spellcasting. Jhedophar is an 18th-level spellcaster. His spellcasting ability is Intelligence (spell save DC 20 , +12 to hit with spell attacks). Jhedophar has the following spells prepared:

Cantrips (at will): *mage hand, minor illusion, prestidigitation, ray of frost*
1st level (4 slots): *burning hands, charm person, magic missile, shield, thunderwave*
2nd level (3 slots): *acid arrow, detect thoughts, invisibility, mirror image*
3rd level (3 slots): *counterspell, dispel magic, fireball, slow*
4th level (3 slots): *blight, dimension door*
5th level (3 slots): *cloudkill, scrying, wall of stone*
6th level (1 slot): *disintegrate, globe of invulnerability*

7th level (1 slot): *delayed blast fireball, plane shift*
8th level (1 slot): *dominate monster, incendiary cloud*
9th level (1 slot): *time stop*
Special Equipment. Jhedophar possesses the *mandrake staff*[A], a *spell scroll* of *power word kill*, a *spell scroll* of *meteor storm*, a *spell scroll* of *prismatic spray*, *boots of striding and springing*, and a *golden circlet of skeleton warrior control*[A].

Actions

Mandrake Staff. Melee Weapon Attack: +15 to hit, reach 5 ft., one target. *Hit*: 9 (1d6 + 6) bludgeoning damage.

Legendary Actions

All standard lich legendary actions plus:
Mandrake Staff **(costs 2 actions).** Jhedophar attacks with the mandrake staff or uses any of its other abilities, including spellcasting.

LARTUGI

Small humanoid (halfling), chaotic evil

Armor Class 18 (*+1 studded leather armor*)
Hit Points 71 (11d8 + 22)
Speed 25 ft.

STR	DEX	CON	INT	WIS	CHA
10 (+0)	20 (+5)	14 (+2)	14 (+2)	10 (+0)	8 (–1)

Saving Throws Dex +8, Int +5
Skills Acrobatics +11, Perception +6, Sleight of Hand +11, Stealth +11
Senses passive Perception 18
Languages Common, Halfling, thieves' cant
Challenge 6 (2,300 XP)

Lucky. When he rolls a 1 on an attack roll, ability check, or saving throw, Lartugi can reroll the die and must use the new roll.
Brave. Lartugi has advantage on saving throws against being frightened.
Nimble. Lartugi can move through the space of any creature that is of a size larger than his.
Cunning Action. Lartugi can take a bonus action on each of his turns in combat. The action can only be used to take the Dash, Disengage, or Hide action.
Evasion. When Lartugi is subjected to an effect that allows him to make a Dexterity saving throw to take only half damage, he instead takes no damage if he succeeds on the saving throw, and only half damage if he fails.
Uncanny Dodge. When an attacker that he can see hits Lartugi with an attack, he can use his reaction to halve the attack's damage against him.
Sneak Attack. Once per turn, Lartugi deals an extra 6d6 damage to one creature he hits with an attack if he has advantage on the attack roll. He does not need advantage on the attack roll if another enemy of the target is within 5 feet of it, that enemy isn't incapacitated, and Lartugi does not have disadvantage on the attack roll.
Supreme Sneak. Lartugi has advantage on a Dexterity (Stealth) check if he moves no more than half his speed on the same turn.
Potion of Speed. Lartugi possesses a *potion of speed*.

Actions

+1 Shortsword. Melee Weapon Attack: +9 to hit, reach 5 ft., one target. *Hit*: 9 (1d6 + 6) piercing damage.

LORD TORK

Medium undead, lawful good

Armor Class 24 (*+2 plate mail armor, +2 shield*)
Hit Points 142 (19d10 + 38)
Speed 40 ft. (with *boots of striding and springing*)

STR	DEX	CON	INT	WIS	CHA
19 (+4)	12 (+1)	15 (+2)	11 (+0)	14 (+2)	10 (+0)

Saving Throws Con +7, Dex +6, Wis +7
Skills Animal Handling +7, Athletics +9, Acrobatics +6, Perception +7
Damage Resistances cold, necrotic
Damage Immunities poison; bludgeoning, slashing and piercing from nonmagical attacks
Condition Immunities charmed, exhaustion, frightened, paralyzed, poisoned
Senses darkvision 60 ft., passive Perception 17
Languages Common
Challenge 15 (13,000 XP)

Boots of Striding and Springing. Lord Tork wears boots of *striding and springing*
Dueling. When he is wielding a melee weapon in one hand and no other weapons, Lord Tork gains a +2 bonus to damage rolls with that weapon.
Find Circlet. Lord Tork can track and find the possessor of his circlet unerringly, as though guided by *locate object* spell with unlimited range. Using this ability, he can also find the last person to possess its circlet.
Frightful Presence. Each creature that is within 60 feet of Lord Tork and aware of him must succeed on a DC 19 Wisdom saving throw or become frightened for 1 minute. A creature can repeat the saving throw at the end of each of its turns, ending the effect on itself on a success. If a creature's saving throw is successful or the effect ends for it, the creature is immune to Lord Tork's Frightful Presence for the next 24 hours.
Gauntlets of Ogre Power. Lord Tork wears *gauntlets of ogre power* giving him the Strength of 19 shown above.
Indomitable. Twice per day, Lord Tork may reroll a failed saving throw. He must use the new roll.
Magic Resistance. Lord Tork has advantage on all saving throws against spells and other magical effects.
Superior Critical. Lord Tork's weapon attacks score a critical hit on a roll of 18–20.
Turn Resistance. Lord Tork has advantage on saving throws against any effect that turns undead.

Actions

Multiattack. Lord Tork makes three Karelis attacks.
Karelis. Melee Weapon Attack: +12 to hit, reach 5 ft., one target. *Hit*: 13 (1d8 + 7) slashing damage,
Necklace of Fireballs. Lord Tork hurls one or more of the 7 beads from his *necklace of fireballs*.

Bonus Actions

Disarm. Lord Tork makes an attack with *Karelis* against a
foe wielding a melee weapon. If he hits, he deals damage as
normal, and the foe must succeed on a Strength saving throw
(using Lord Tork's attack roll as its DC) or drop its weapon.

MOHRG

Medium undead, chaotic evil

Armor Class 12
Hit Points 112 (15d8 + 45)
Speed 30 ft.

STR	DEX	CON	INT	WIS	CHA
18 (+4)	14 (+2)	17 (+3)	11 (+0)	10 (+0)	8 (−1)

Damage Immunities poison
Condition Immunities charmed, exhaustion, frightened,
paralyzed, petrified, poisoned, stunned
Senses darkvision 60ft., passive Perception 10
Languages —
Challenge 8 (3,900 XP)

Create Spawn. Any humanoid creature slain by the mohrg
rises as a zombie at the beginning of the mohrg's next turn.
If this occurs, the mohrg regains up to 10 hit points, and the
morhg can immediately make one slam attack as a reaction.

Actions

Multiattack. The mohrg makes two Slam attacks and one
Tongue attack.
Slam. *Melee Weapon Attack:* +7 to hit, reach 5 ft., one target.
Hit: 13 (2d8 + 4) bludgeoning damage, and the target is
grappled and restrained (escape DC15), and the morhg can't
grapple another creature or use its slam attack.
Tongue. *Melee Weapon Attack:* +7 to hit, reach 5 ft., one
target. *Hit:* The target must make a DC 16 Constitution
saving throw. On a failed save, the target takes 21 (6d6)
necrotic damage and is paralyzed for 1 minute. The creature
can repeat the saving throw at the end of each of its turns,
ending the effect on a success.

RAT, SHADOW

Tiny undead, unaligned

Armor Class 12
Hit Points 7 (2d4 + 2)
Speed 30 ft., climb 15 ft.

STR	DEX	CON	INT	WIS	CHA
4 (−3)	14 (+2)	12 (+1)	2 (−4)	10 (+0)	6 (−2)

Skills Stealth +4 (+6 in dim light or darkness)
Damage Vulnerabilities radiant
Damage Resistances acid, cold, fire, lightning
Damage Immunities necrotic, poison
Condition Immunities exhaustion, frightened, grappled,
paralyzed, petrified, poisoned, prone, restrained
Senses darkvision 60 ft., passive Perception 10
Languages —
Challenge 1/4 (50 XP)

Amorphous. The shadow rat can move through a space as
narrow as 1 inch wide without squeezing.
Shadow Stealth. While in dim light or darkness, the shadow
rat can take the Hide action as a bonus action.
Sunlight Weakness. While in sunlight, the shadow rat has
disadvantage on attack rolls, ability checks, and saving throws.

Actions

Bite. *Melee Weapon Attack:* +4 to hit, reach 5 ft., one creature.
Hit: 4 (1d4 + 2) necrotic damage. If the target is not undead,
its Strength score is reduced by 1d4. The target dies if this
reduces its Strength score to 0. Otherwise, the reduction
lasts until the target finishes a short or long rest.

TRAPPER

Huge aberration, unaligned

Armor Class 17 (natural armor)
Hit Points 126 (12d12 + 48)
Speed 10 ft.

STR	DEX	CON	INT	WIS	CHA
20 (+5)	12 (+1)	18 (+4)	11 (+0)	12 (+1)	9 (−1)

Skills Perception +4, Stealth +4
Damage Resistances cold, fire; slashing or piercing from
nonmagical attacks
Condition Immunities blinded, charmed, deafened,
exhaustion, frightened, prone
Senses blindsight 60 ft. (blind beyond this radius), passive
Perception 15
Languages —
Challenge 7 (2,900 XP)

Ooze Form. The trapper has no vital organs and is immune to
extra critical hit damage and damage from a Sneak Attack.
Damage Transfer. While it is grappling a creature, the
trapper takes only half the damage dealt to it (rounded
down), and that creature takes the other half.
False Appearance. While the trapper remains motionless,
it is indistinguishable from the floor of a room or cavern
(including a box/chest if the trapper chooses to emulate such
an object).

Actions

Multiattack. The trapper makes one Buffet attack and uses
Smother.
Buffet. *Melee Weapon Attack:* +8 to hit, reach 10 ft., one
creature. *Hit:* 18 (3d8 + 5) bludgeoning damage, and the
target is grappled (escape DC 18). Until the grapple ends,
the target is restrained, has disadvantage on Strength
checks and Strength saving throws, and the trapper cannot
grapple or Buffet another target.
Smother. The trapper wraps itself around one creature it has
grappled of Large size or smaller, completely enclosing it.
The smothered target is restrained, blinded, no longer able
to speak or use spells with verbal components, and it cannot
breathe. At the start of each of the trapper's turns, the target
takes 18 (3d8 + 5) bludgeoning damage.